# The Secret at Gray Mountain

SALLY KAMMERER

Copyright © 2020 Sally Kammerer
All rights reserved
First Edition

PAGE PUBLISHING, INC.
Conneaut Lake, PA

First originally published by Page Publishing 2020

ISBN 978-1-64701-214-4 (pbk)
ISBN 978-1-64701-215-1 (digital)

Printed in the United States of America

# Chapter 1

Her hair was a shock of long black ribbon that curled down her backside. Her eyes mirrored the blue of the sky above as she stood on tiptoe to peer over the fence line at the sandy haired boy in blue jeans and a faded T-shirt. He was hauling boxes in and out of the yellow house just one house down from her neighbors. A smile graced her lips and her heart fluttered old enough at eleven to have a serious crush but nowhere near old enough to know what to do with it or what it all meant. Loud barking and a snarling fur face leapt toward her, knocking her back hard on her butt.

"Damn it, Michael, how many times have I told you to not lean on my fence?"

Mrs. June was a hard-faced woman whom Michael swore was born with a permanent scowl on her face. For most of her entire life, she had been nothing but a thorn in her side. Michael stood up and stuck her tongue out in defiance. She could hear her mother's voice: "That's not how we treat others—kindness is the best medicine..."

"It's Jane, Mrs. June. My name is Jane!"

Michael stomped her foot for emphasis. She had never been able to get it across to anyone to call her by her middle name, which she learned was far more feminine than her given name. Mrs. June laughed and pulled the dog back down off the fence, petting him softly. Her eyes shot to where Michael had been looking not ten seconds before.

"Ah, new neighbors. More kids—great. Stay off the fence—last warning!"

Mrs. June turned back for her house, and Michael stuck her tongue out, waggling her fingers in her ears at her backside. Suddenly, she felt a red rush to her cheeks and looked across the fence to see the boy staring at her. Their eyes locked, not much distance in the small square of lawn separating them. Meeting his smile, she shrunk back in embarrassment, running up the back porch and slamming the screen door behind her. A baby let out a long short wail somewhere down the hall, and Michael closed her eyes and sank against the wall waiting for it.

"Michael Jane, what did I tell you about slamming that door when you came in this house!"

Michael grumbled under her breath.

"Not to…"

She followed the sound of the crying baby and her mother's voice past two small bedrooms that mirrored each other split by a small bathroom and set of stairs that led to two more bedrooms on the second floor and a modest half bath. The hall opened to a large kitchen and front room open to each other, fans whirred in the stuffy unairconditioned space, and drapes were pulled across large windows. Her mother was drying dishes, and the smell of breakfast still lingered in the air. Her Aunt Carol snuggled a small red-faced baby that had begun to quiet on an overstuffed old brown sofa. There were two mismatched chairs and a TV humming on low and a few small squat bookshelves made up the room.

"Where's Danny?"

Michael pulled a chair up to the table and munched on a leftover biscuit.

"Working with your father today."

Her brother was a good five years older than her, and the difference was striking. Although they had little in common, she still adored him, and he had a soft spot for her as well. It had been the four of them for up until a year ago when her Aunt Carol showed up one Christmas pregnant and nowhere to go and her mother had graciously offered her a place to crash till she got back on her feet. Michael was okay with the arrangement till her cousin was born a few short months later. As cute as she was, she was nothing but a nuisance, crying at all hours of the day and night, and then her mother laid into her every time she so much as sneezed, and it had only been six whole days!

"We have new neighbors in the yellow house by Mrs. June."

Her mother wiped her hands on a dish rag and turned around. Her hair was the same jet black as her daughter's but had begun to gray softly at the roots. Small wrinkles danced around her blue eyes, and her lithe frame had softened by thirty pounds or so between children and age but Michael still thought she was the prettiest woman alive.

"Oh...well, do they have children?"

Michael swallowed the last bite of biscuit.

"I saw a boy."

Her mother kissed the top of her head and collected the last of the dishes.

"You should go say hello then. I'll introduce myself later when I get this cleaned up."

Michael grumbled and headed to the living room and flopped down in a chair, letting it rock back and forth, banging her feet against it, getting looks from Aunt Carrol as the soft thudding vibrated the room. All Michael could think as Aunt Carrol laid the baby down in a bassinet nearby finally peacefully asleep was, *Well, she best get used to it. I was here first.*

Instead, she grinned and said, "Have you named her yet?"

Aunt Carrol sank down to the sofa with a tired smile; she looked awfully cross. Having babies from her list, Michael thought, she wondered how her mom and Aunt Carrol were even sisters. She was a good ten years younger and had soft strawberry blond hair and brown eyes.

"No, not yet, have any ideas?"

She had to admit minus the baby, Aunt Carrol was pretty cool and let her get away with stuff her mom didn't.

"Just don't give her a boy name like Michael," she stage-whispered.

Her mother snapped the towel and interrupted. Walking over, she sat down on the chair opposite Michael with a heavy sigh. "There is a good story for that, and I can guarantee you're not the only girl named Michael."

She made a face at her mom.

"You could at least call me by my middle name. Instead the whole world knows me as Michael."

Her mother grinned. "Your name helps you stand out. It will take you lots of places, darling. Trust me."

Michael let out a sigh and jumped to her feet. "I'm going to ride my bike."

Aunt Carrol looked lovingly at the baby. "I think I'll name her Julie."

Michael nodded in approval. Her mother caught her arm before she bolted out the door. "I'm bringing your father and brother lunch and then shopping later. Should I find you?"

She shrugged. "Nah."

"All right then, stay out of trouble and be back by this afternoon or I'm hunting you down."

Michael slammed through the front door, receiving a hush from both women in her life. She picked up her bike where it lay on the front lawn and sped away down past the houses, rushing past the yellow house in what she hoped was a blur before turning around and going back slower so she could spy on the new boy.

"Hey, boy!"

Michael stopped her bike by the white picket fence and looked right at him as he came back out for another box or two, she was sure. He paused and wiped sweat from his brow; he grinned back at her.

"What's your name?"

He strode forward and extended his hand. "Chris."

Michael took notice of the scuffed brown cowboy boots. "Nice boots."

Chris chuckled. "Thanks...I think."

She stared hard at him for a long, piercing second. "I'm Michael. I know it's a boy's name, but that's what my mom gave me, so I don't want to hear it." She offered him her best scrunch face. "I'm eleven in four days. I'm no little girl, boy!"

He laughed again, and she hated to admit she liked it a little. "Well, Michael, it's nice to meet you. Now it's best if you run along and play—my momma is gonna have my head if I don't get this truck unloaded by noon."

She stuck her tongue out at him and sped away as fast as her legs would carry her. The warm summer breeze whipped deliciously around her. Her ears perked as she heard her name in the distance being called. The world began to spin and blur, and suddenly…the voice broke me straight out of the dream and I sat up, half expecting to be back in that tiny house along that street where I had killed many summer afternoons riding my bike, lying amidst a sea of stuffed unicorns and teddy bears.

"You better answer me or I'm—"

I popped out of bed and ran to the door, swinging it open before she could bust it in with her foot.

"Mmmmm, I'm up. I swear—"

Maria stood in her dark-blue patrol uniform. Her deep mahogany skin and short curvy frame often invited some trouble from the male side, but I had known her since my college days, and she didn't let it get the best of her. Fresh out of the academy, she was a tough cookie, and she was damn good at what she did.

"Must have been some dream?" She winked at me and rattled her car keys. "Gotta run, see you tonight?"

I rubbed sleep from my eyes. "Yeah, thanks for waking me."

"Anytime."

Some dream, you could say that again. It was one of those dreams that didn't come that often, where you woke up but it still felt as real as a memory from the other day. The remnants of the dream filtered in and out of my mind. As a therapist, I had to pull it apart to search for any relevant meaning; of course, I could find none.

"Get it together!" I told myself, as I used the facilities, clipped my hair back, and headed back to my bedroom, checking the clock on my nightstand. I had just enough time to apply some makeup and choose a gray linen pantsuit I paired with a pair of pearls and slightly heeled pair of black boots. I hurried down the steps and across the two front rooms of the small two-bedroom town house I shared with Maria. Casual friends already, we happened to be living under the same roof by separate coincidences in our life—hers was moving out of a dorm room and mine was moving out of my now ex-boyfriend's house. Over coffee a year ago, we put our situations and our pocketbooks together and decided on the best solution was going in on a rental together. With opposing schedules and like-mindedness, so far, it had worked out brilliantly for the most part.

# Chapter 2

My office was a square box across town and a few blocks from the University of Washington, tucked between restaurants offering cheap, quick lunches. I was blasted by the smell of frying oils and savory breads, as I parked in a small lot across the street and hurried out of the morning chill. The office was nothing to boast about, but this small piece of real estate was bought and paid for by yours truly. The two-year-old black therapy group was my pride and joy. Besides the accountant I kept on the side for taxes, my only other employee I had hired six months ago to keep my ever-fluctuating calendar in check was Debra, and she had been a godsend from day one. Bells clattered as I stepped inside and flipped the sign over to open. Debra had taken the small couple hundred square foot front room from a tight unwelcoming space to something quite inviting. She had picked up some rust-colored armchairs and an old olive-green antique sofa that gave the perfect Seattle vibe. A table-sized fountain bubbled on an end table by a carefully placed glass lamp, where fresh magazines and papers were spread across the polished antique coffee table.

"Good morning, Miss Black."

I smiled at her. She sat manning a laptop and a phone behind a matching antique desk, old enough to be my mother. She always came neatly dressed in slacks and blouses, her gray hair pinned back from a lovely oval face, smelling of lilacs. A coffee machine hummed nearby on another end table.

"Thanks for the formality…ah, you got one 'I love you…'"

She laughed a bubbly sound as I made my way over to the keurig and nearly gave it a kiss. I chose a dark roast selection from the wire basket and made a quick cup, complete with cream and most likely a tad too much sugar, before heading back to my office. Just down a short hall, past a white tile and black metal bathroom, Debra had appointed a Paris theme here with cute matching toiletry items. I wondered idly if she had been a designer in another life as I unlocked my office door, a slab of antique cherry wood that added to the ambience. I walked into a small square of blue-carpeted space just big enough for the traditional setup, a small desk and laptop in one corner, a slate-gray modern last-minute purchase that I hoped to trade in for something trendier one of these days, and a white wood-framed window that showcased a soft rose-colored loveseat and a matching armchair. I had added to the ambience with a few throw pillows, their tassels worn down from nervous fingers, and blankets. Low lamplight added to the welcoming atmosphere, and there were plenty of tissue boxes. A small low book shelf took up the last corner and was mostly texts from my college days at the nearby university. Into my early thirties, I had buckled down right out of high school and had not come up for air for the last ten years, going from a bachelor's degree in psych to a master's in social work to round out my degree and give me the most flexibility.

After my graduation date, I had accepted a position at the place I had done my practicum at, finding it a necessary and blessed transition. My goal from the beginning was not just to help others but to be my own boss, so to speak. I had saved a lot of pennies and burned a lot of bridges socially and romantically in order to get to this place, and now I was finding myself at the top, looking down and feeling like I was missing out on a whole lot of something, a whole lot of life. The honest truth was that I had spent so many years helping others I had deserted my own life, and it was now a hot mess on many levels.

I sank down to the small chair behind the desk and checked my work phone for messages although Debra had done a good job taking care of those recently. Taking the moment to catch my breath before my first patient of the day, I found my mind wandering as I mused over the dream I had earlier. I wondered idly why that boy's face had come into my mind after so many years. Chris and I had grown up together and, for a brief moment in our youth, tried on a romantic union, but that had crashed and burned as often does in the wreckage of inexperienced youth. Over the years, most defiantly, when I found myself back in that old neighborhood having dinner at my moms, I occasionally wondered as you would an old friend how he was doing, what had become of his life. Going back there to that place, well, the psychological part of my brain couldn't help but analyze it.

"Come in."

A sudden knock at my door interrupted my runaway thought train, and a tall, broad-shouldered middle-aged man with gray hair swept back from a kind face stepped in. Tom had been a patient for a little over two months, coming to me for chronic depression, and who could blame him? His wife of over thirty years had recently passed from cancer. I had few grief cases under my belt but readily accepted the referral from his primary doctor. I was wondering from our first appointment how reluctant Tom would be. He was an old-fashioned sort of guy who reminded me a lot of my father, kind and strong, not one to take help but relied on his own wits.

Tom had surprised me in a good way. He was eager to talk about his lovely wife and their years of blessed marriage—some good and some definite trials. I played the therapist and tried to encourage tools to help with his grief, but mostly, in the hour we spent together, he was happy just to share, and sharing seemed to be what he needed most.

"Tom, how are you doing today?"

"All right, I suppose…"

Tom sank down in his usual spot on the corner of the sofa; his fingers drummed a soundless tune on the armrest.

"What would you like to talk about today, Tom?"

Loraine was never far from his mind, and as he talked about a new group of widowers he had joined at his church and how the support seemed to help, he began to knit in more stories of how he had met his wife, how young and beautiful she seemed, how poetic their love story had been.

# Chapter 3

Once upon a time there had been as much poetry in my story as there had been in Loraine and Toms, but unlike their story, what started was never finished. I had been a young idealistic teenager then, caught up in the charismatic ways of best my friend, and what better place than to write a love story but in the arms of someone who knew you better than you knew yourself? Ever since that afternoon, I had sped up to his place on my white and pink bike and threw myself into his life. We had become fast friends; despite our age difference, we looked out for one another. What often happens did with me, and one summer, the remnants of any little girl I had been drifted away and I began to turn into the woman I was today, and as I entered my freshman year of high school, Chris started his senior year, and something changed that warm autumn night, something that had possibly been brewing for a long time.

> "Hey, Cowboy…" I murmured close to him, so close I could feel his heartbeat. He gazed down at me with those gray green eyes I loved so much. I could feel my family's eyes boring a hole in my backside.
> 
> "Well, look at you…"
> 
> His smile widened, and I felt my heart trip a couple beats. I had never felt so alive as I did in that very moment. I had asked the boy next door, my very best friend, to my homecoming dance.

He had had a few already, but this was the first we would attend together. I felt myself nearly turn red, and I could only imagine why in fact I felt a bit foolish standing there in the driveway of my house. Every particle of my being wanted to dash back inside. Chris had never seen me out of a pair of blue jeans and a tee. In that moment, I stood before him in a crimson knee-length dress, my black hair pinned back. My mom had carefully helped me do my makeup, mixes of soft floral pinks.

"You look beautiful." His voice was a whisper, and I felt the roughness of his hand trace the smoothness of my cheek, and my heart caught in my throat as our eyes met, and I had never wanted something as badly as I wanted to kiss him in that moment.

"Have her home by ten." My father's voice echoed nearby from where he stood guard on the porch, and I jumped a bit in my own skin, forgetting for a moment he was even still there.

"Leave her be…" I heard my mother's voice counter my father's, and we both giggled as we turned to wave at my parents and got into Chris's truck, the gravel of the drive crunching under the tires as he turned out onto the main road and headed for my high school gym.

"Thank you for tonight."

I dared to touch his leg, and he startled me by pulling off the main drag and onto the river road; we bounced along the gravel for a bit before he stopped the truck. It was a cloudless night, and the velvet sky was a blanket of glistening diamonds. The air rustled in from open windows, warm and soft on my skin, and I looked at him, my face a mask of confusion.

"Listen, Michael, there is something I need to talk to you about." I looked at him, my heart doing a funny flutter in my chest, and I spoke just to ease the silence. "Maybe we should forget the dance. I don't know why I got dressed up in the first place—you know I'm not that kind of girl."

I looked away from him then and felt his hand catch my arm gently so my gaze was brought back to his, and suddenly without any warning, his lips swept down across mine, and I felt my breath catch and my eyes slip closed, and for a second that seemed ageless, I melted against him; I felt as if my whole body was sighing.

"I'm sorry, maybe that was too soon…" he murmured as he pulled back suddenly.

The memory traversed my thoughts as I threaded my way through the rush of Friday traffic, eager to get home after a long work week and finally relax. Remnants of the dream from last night filtered in, and I wondered idly why I found myself so intensely time traveling down memory lane, why this man who had not been a part of my life for a long time, who popped in now and then in my memories, suddenly was so much on my mind.

# Chapter 4

"What are you doing here?"

I almost found myself snapping when I saw him standing on my porch as I walked up, my arms loaded with sacks of groceries. It was just a quarter after seven, and I was looking forward to spending a Friday evening in with the "girls." I had all the fixings for tacos and a bottle of tequila for margaritas, and no man was standing in the way of that, most particularly this man.

"Well, hello to you too."

I looked over him, his brown hair rumpled, a five-o'-clock shadow on his square handsome face. His brown eyes seemed light and melty, suggesting he had something ticking in that brain his he needed to unload.

"Don't do that."

I laughed and stepped in front of him, thrusting the groceries in his arms so I could unlock the door. "Do what, Richard?"

He laughed in return and followed me inside to the kitchen. "Read me like that. Everything is fine. If I wanted a therapist, I would pay for one. I didn't come here for that."

*Oh really?* I thought to myself. This man had been in my life for the better part of the last decade, through the good, the bad, and the ugly. Once upon a time, we had been good friends, so good we too often ended up in bed together, and one crazy night a little over a year ago, we decided if we were sharing a bed, we might as well enter a relationship and not only announced our status as boyfriend and girlfriend but took it a step further and moved into the same domicile together. As you can imagine, that worked out fabulously, and after a nasty breakup, we were slowly collecting the pieces and trying desperately for whatever reason to salvage our friendship. I motioned for him to set the groceries on the butcher block island in the center of the kitchen. The townhouse was well set up for entering its large kitchen complete with an island overlooked the most efficient living room and dining space one could imagine. I headed to the fridge and pulled out a beer and popped the top, sliding it his way. He grabbed the bottle, took a sip, and sank down to a barstool.

"I'm sorry if I seemed rude earlier. It's been a long week…looking forward to a girls' night in."

I glanced at the clock on the wall.

"You have exactly forty-five minutes."

I grinned and began sorting and chopping veggies in front of him.

"I'll send you a check in the mail. Seriously, I didn't come here to get the third degree or ruin the night for you."

"You sell real estate—how bad can it be?"

Richard took a long swallow off the beer as I sliced onions. "I found a body today."

I looked up at him suddenly and felt the tip of the knife blade pierce my skin. "Shit!"

I pulled back and nursed my injured thumb; Richard looked at me in concern.

"I'm fine, just a scratch…" I snatched a paper towel and wrapped it around my thumb. "What do you mean, you found a body…?"

Richard spun the beer bottle, obviously perplexed in thought. "I have seen some things in my years of service, Michael, but this… this was different in a way and a lot more blood than that."

He grinned awkwardly and motioned toward my finger. I didn't find it amusing and rummaged through drawers till I found a Band-Aid.

"What the hell, Richard? Maybe you need a therapist. What the hell happened? What are you talking about?"

I wrapped my thumb and came back over to clean the cutting board.

"I was checking an empty property, getting ready for a client to come by. I went around back and there it was, bottom of the empty pool."

Richard shook his head and washed his face with his hands.

"I don't know what happened to that poor guy, but it was brutal. He painted a good part of that cement red. I called the police—they were combing the area, fuck, the whole damn neighborhood. I just can't seem to put it out of my head. I just wanted to talk to you, to see you."

I sighed and looked at him. I wanted to be friends with him. I wanted to go back to the days before we had crossed the friend line and found ourselves first in bed and then taking a stab at the domestic thing and me moving in. What had seemed like a good idea at the time fell apart rather quickly, and now, just six weeks later, we were both desperately trying to find our way back to the remains of our friendship, and part of that, I wanted to point out in that moment, was boundaries.

"Richard…"

"Say no more. I'll leave you to your evening."

Richard glanced at the clock just as Maria came in the front door. She smiled warmly at him and threw me a questioning stare. I shrugged.

"I was just on my way out…"

I opened my mouth to say something, and he cut me off, touching my arm and kissing my cheek gently. I grabbed him back before he could go.

"Hey, call me later please. I say that not just as a therapist but a friend, okay? I mean it."

"I will. Maria."

As soon as the door closed, my best friend was all over me. "What the hell is he doing here?"

I went back to chopping onions. "I'm sure you heard the buzz on the radio…?"

She shrugged at me. "Police activity?"

"Yep, house Richard was showing in Medina…"

Maria undid the clip in her hair, and her deep brown locks unraveled to her shoulders, framing her face.

"Not my jurisdiction. Besides, I'm stuck mostly with traffic—speeding tickets, parking violations…"

I laughed and pointed the utensil her way. "You will get there one day."

"Anyways back to Medina…"

"Richard found a body…"

"Like a dead body? Shit, that must have been something. I'll have to see what I can find out, if anything. Most likely, not more than the news anchors would know in my lowly position. Damn, poor Richard. I can see why he was so shook up."

I tossed the onions in a pan and set the temp to low; I pulled out some fresh chopped chicken and added it to the mix.

"Go get changed. Audrey and Janette should be here in the next thirty—something about kids and bedtime but they should be here."

## Chapter 5

The night had unfolded like a black carpet, and wisps of soft clouds released a mist of rain as Richard climbed into his antique cream-colored Mercedes from the early seventies, long before he was born, but still he always treasured relics, and maybe that's how he got into real estate, always seeing the potential in front of him. Regardless of what had led him there, he knew what had made him stay, and that was the lure of bigger and better properties and the persuasion of the all-mighty dollar. He had done well over the years for himself, he supposed. He sold houses in the greater Seattle area, was well known among those in the industry, made a decent income, and owned a house in Queen Ann. Sitting on one of many gentle slopes, its front yard was sections of terraced rock wall that sprang to life, every spring in several different shades of reds, pinks, blues, and orange poppies and tulips, for now scraggly shrubs and small lamps lit the staircase that wound up to the front door, a curious shade of turquoise, one of Michael's contributions in the short time she had lived here.

Parking along the street near the detached the garage in bad need of repair, the house was a far cry from the luxury real estate he sold, but it was comfy and a place to call home. The place had been a fixer-upper when he had landed it, and he took each repair as a slow, gentle hobby. As he stepped inside, his footsteps echoing off the hardwood floors, he flicked on lamps, lending a soft yellow glow that cast shadows across slate-gray walls. A charcoal-colored sofa and matching armchairs took up the small front living room, where they were artfully set to face the fireplace. Once a wood-burning red brick monstrosity, he had dialed it down with white paint and a wood-lacquered mantel.

Kicking off shoes and tossing his tie and jacket across a chair, he headed through a rounded archway into a small room just big enough for a dining room table and four chairs, a mess of papers, and his laptop. It served as a good office. The kitchen was through the second archway and still sported the seventies-style olive-green linoleum. The cabinets had been painted a fresh white, and the outdated appliances had been replaced by stainless steel; it was a work in progress, to say the least. Standing at the fridge with the door open, he contemplated the idea of food and reached for a second beer; his stomach had still not caught up to his brain. His cellphone buzzed in his pocket, interrupting any further thoughts.

"Hello…?"

Richard headed back to the living room where he sank against the welcoming cushions of the sofa.

"Mr. Jackson?"

"Speaking."

"Sorry to bother you so late at night, sir, but we need you to come down to the station to make a statement."

The afternoon he had flashed through his mind. "Already gave a statement to the police, sir."

"I understand that, Mr. Jackson, but we need it on record."

Great—as if his day couldn't get worse, he knew he was a suspect. "I don't know what else I can tell you. I'm—"

"Can you come in first thing in the morning, say nine a.m.?"

Richard sighed. As if he really had a choice in the matter, he thought idly. "Sure, I'll be there."

## Chapter 6

I yawned and rubbed sleep from my eyes, pulling the robe tighter around me to block out the chill of the morning. My head throbbed lightly from last night's racket but had, for the most part, been a roaring success. I headed downstairs for the kitchen and was glad to smell the aroma of coffee scenting the air.

"You're a lifesaver, Maria."

I headed straight for the coffee pot and fished out my best cup from the cupboard, white and red with the letters reading *Faith* in cursive. I filled it nearly to the top and added in vanilla creamer. I headed for the living room, where I found Maria dressed and eating cereal and drinking coffee.

"On shift today?"

I nursed my cup, wrapping my hands around it and soaking in the warmth. I took a large swallow, relishing the taste. I sank down into an armchair across from the sofa, my eyes catching the news on the TV.

"Always the life of a rookie…"

I chuckled and turned my eyes to the TV. Weather faded away to an update, and as the picture spun into full view, taking up the entire screen, my heart froze in my chest. The unswallowed coffee came flying out, soaking the front of my tee. I made a quick choking noise and found Maria's full attention on me, her brown eyes suddenly wide in surprise.

"Are you okay…?"

I motioned for her to turn it up and leaned forward to listen intently to the newscaster.

"Police are asking for anyone with any information to come forward. A body found at a local Medina home yesterday afternoon has been identified as fifty-eight-year-old James Jefferson…"

I wiped coffee off myself and set the cup down.

"I know him. I know that man he is. He was a patient. I haven't seen him in eight months, but I treated him for nearly a year."

Maria turned down the TV as it faded away to another story.

"Looks like you have a phone call to make."

"You think? It may not be relevant at all, and what information can I give them?"

Maria got up and headed for the kitchen. "Wait long enough, they will be pounding on your door."

"There goes my Saturday. Please tell me if you hear anything else on the radar."

"Will do, but like I said, different jurisdictions, don't think I will. Anyways I gotta run. Maybe see you tonight?"

"Yep."

As the door shut behind Maria, I got up to clean myself off, which included a shower. My mind buzzed with the newest information, and then Richard came slamming into my mind. Was the world really that small a place? How could some old client of mine be randomly murdered and dumped at a house of someone I knew pretty damn well?

\*\*\*

"I told you, that's all I know…"

Richard sat uncomfortably on one side of a metal table in a room with no windows, but he was damn sure he was being watched and perhaps even recorded. Suddenly, he wondered if he needed a lawyer.

"Sir, you do have to understand the impartiality of the situation?"

The detective pushed rust-colored hair back from a square clean-shaven face and slapped the file folder and a notepad and pen in front of him, taking the other seat, making the bulk of his body and his gaze leave Richard to question the authenticity of his story.

"So you showed up at a quarter after three to wait for a client to arrive for a three-thirty appointment?"

Richard sighed. "Yes, that's correct."

"You then checked the property…front and back?"

Richard sighed again, trying to keep his cool. "Yes, and like I said that's when I discovered the body lying there like that. Geezus, what a mess. Do you have an idea of who it was?"

"Why don't you tell me…?"

The detective opened the folder and shoved it across the desk. The man in the picture was not a bloody mess and stared back at him, making his stomach turn—gray eyes, slightly grayer hair, wide smile, one arm missing because the photo had been cropped and enhanced, and he knew exactly who was standing on the missing side.

"Shit!"

"Care to change your story, Mr. Jackson?"

Richard ran his fingers through his hair as Michael quickly came to mind in all the chaos. How had the one man who had helped him build his name in real estate that he had referred to Michael once wound up on his property? If he felt unsure about being watched before, he felt for sure he was being watched now.

"I didn't recognize him then, but yeah…damn, he was a good guy."

Richard picked up the glossy five-by-seven print, ran a thumb across it, and handed it back. "I'll do whatever you ask, but I didn't have a damn thing to do with his death. In fact, I hadn't seen him in three months. Last time we chatted, it was all business, a couple properties he was throwing my way. We met for a quick lunch to go over the houses. He was happy, talked about jetting off to Mexico for the week with some girl he was dating at the time…but he was a good guy. Got to know him when I started selling real estate in his area a couple years back. Thought he wanted to shave off any competition, but he was a great guy, sort of took me under his wing."

"So you were good friends then?"

"I can't say that. It was more just business. Saw him every couple months, chatted on the phone a few times, called to ask him for advice, but we didn't really hang out. We weren't best buds or anything…"

"What else can you tell me about Mr. Jefferson?"

Richard sighed and pushed the photo back. "Believe me, I wish I could tell you more, but we mostly talked shop. Occasionally, he would talk about some girl he was dating or something he had bought or some adventure he had gone on."

"Boasting?"

"Maybe a little, but mostly I think he was trying to encourage me. Really, he was a happy guy…"

"Any enemies you know of?"

"No…"

Silence entered the room like a death note, and finally the detective pulled the file back and sat back against his chair with a heavy sigh.

"I will let you go, but only because I have nothing to hold you."

Their eyes crossed, and Richard took that as a threat and not a warning. Getting up and grabbing his jacket, he headed out of the station and into the cool, crisp fall air. He thought of Michael but in a completely different way and wondered if she knew. Hell, probably half the city knew by now, but what he was about to tell her, had to tell her, could be a major deal breaker.

# Chapter 7

I headed into my office at around eleven. Even though it was the one Saturday a month I allotted myself time off, I suddenly found myself back at work minus the usual attire. I had pulled my hair back hastily and thrown on a pair of black stretch pants, an oversized sweatshirt, and a pair of tennies that had pounded a lot of pavement, hoping maybe this trip wasn't fruitless and I could squeeze a run in later.

"Mr. Jefferson…"

I pulled his file out, more curious than ever, remembering a strikingly handsome older gentleman, somewhat charming and gregarious but the rest of the details, if any, had left my mind. My phone began to vibrate noisily against the desktop as I flipped the folder open and began to scan through notes. I glanced over, ready to let it go to voice mail when I realized it was Richard.

"Yes, Richard…?"

Sounded like he was driving.

"Where are you at? The connection is a bit choppy?"

"Driving. Did they release the name on the news yet?"

I balked for a second, trying to figure out what the hell he was talking about, and then I caught on.

"Yes, what about him?"

"Where are you at?"

I stopped flipping and listened more intently between crackles.

"Richard, seriously, I can half hear you. I'm in my office…"

No sooner had the words left my mouth than the line went dead, I turned back to the file on hand and began scrolling through notes. Over the next half an hour, I came up with what I had initially come up the first time we had met. James was an overall happy gentleman suffering from a mild case of depression and anxiety, mostly caused from stress and a few failed relationships. We spent sessions talking about ways to reduce stress, goals in life, general stuff, nothing too extravagant. I was another luxury he could afford to have. A sudden pounding on glass interrupted my thoughts and I got up cautiously heading to the front, when I saw Richard standing on the other side, I unlocked the door and let him in.

"What the hell are you doing here? What is going on?"

Richard sighed and shut the door.

"You have to hear me out for a second. There is something I really need to tell you…"

I led him back to my office, and he sank down on the sofa. As I sat back behind the desk, I couldn't help but laugh at the irony of the situation.

"Never thought you would get me on the couch, did ya?"

I waved it off.

"Get back to the point, Richard."

"I was with the police all morning. They were interviewing me again. The victim was James Jefferson."

I looked at him, pretty sure the entire city knew who he was now.

"And this is news how?"

Richard tangled his hands together.

"I knew him—he was, I guess you could say, a work acquaintance…"

I gaped at him.

"I know I referred him to you…"

I sank back into my chair.

"What? Why are you telling me this now, Richard?"

I furrowed my eyebrows at him, my cheeks flushed red with anger, and I could sense he knew. He held up his hand almost as if in defense.

"Michael, come on. Don't shoot the messenger. I really didn't think it mattered."

I sighed and tugged on my ponytail.

"You referred a friend to me for therapy but didn't bother telling me? Let me guess, this is when we were still fucking?"

I shot back, fully irritated now, to imagine he simply hadn't mentioned. The fact he knew me for whatever reason was fine, but the fact he had done it when we shared an abode a bed together seemed even more intolerable.

"Michael, please, I didn't come here for this…"

His brown eyes seemed to be pleading with me, but I wasn't in the mood for it, I crossed my arms and sat back against my chair, letting him know I was listening but fully using my body language to let him know he better tread lightly.

"What was I supposed to do? He was mostly a work acquaintance. What was I supposed to tell him? Hey, my girlfriend's a therapist. Heard you needed one, so yeah, she's a good one."

I loosened my arms a bit and rested my hands on my desk, tapping my nails lightly.

"Listen, you're good at what you do. He mentioned needing or wanting to speak to a therapist. I guess he figured maybe I knew a former client, a friend, I don't know… I didn't want it to get weird. I take it he didn't mention me?"

I sighed as I began to see his point. I couldn't help but see the truth.

"Maybe you had no reason to tell him, but you had a reason to tell me. I hold patient confidentiality at my highest regard. No one's name gets mentioned. You should have…well, you should have trusted me."

A moment washed between us, and I began to realize one of the reasons we had never worked as more than friends, and I began to even question that at the moment.

"Richard?"

He stepped close to the desk.

"Where do we go from here? Not this…"

I tapped the file.

"But us?"

"I hope we can stay friends, Michael, I mean that, but it's up to you. You lead, I'll follow."

I sighed and got up and walked to the office door, opening it for him. He followed, and we stepped outside into a chilly afternoon. I leaned up on my tiptoes and kissed the roughness of his cheek.

"Friends?"

"Friends..." He murmured it back, squeezed my arm gently, and I watched him walk away.

"Looks like rain..." I muttered to no one in particular as I turned and headed back inside to my office, sitting down at my desk and peeling open the file.

"What do you have to say, James...?"

I opened my pile of typed and handwritten notes and began to slowly go through the top layer, my eyes scanning for anything that might jump out at me. The phone once again interrupted my thoughts.

"Hey, Mom, how are you?"

"More like how are *you*?"

I sighed and sank back against my chair. My mom never failed to remind me when it had been too long between phone calls. The fact we stayed pretty good friends and remained on each other's radar quite frequently after all these years was a definite blessing.

"Just busy, Mom. Sorry I haven't called."

"My career girl..."

I could picture her in her favorite chair in the front room on an old rotary phone. She owned a cell but rarely used it. Her black hair had turned a deep gray, and even though she was fifty-two years young, she refused to dye it. Her blue eyes had never changed, and laugh lines touched her face like a soft whisper. I read her mind easily.

"Ok, Mom, I'll try to make dinner tonight..."

She chuckled softly.

"You think that's what I called for?"

I laughed back.

"You're hilarious, Mom. I'll see you around four, okay? Love you..."

"Love you too, baby."

I hung up and checked the clock, grumbling as I realized somehow it was past one in the afternoon. I shut the file and shoved it in my briefcase and headed out just as a cool rain burst through the cloud cover and caused me to be soaked through by the time I made it to my car. With an hour-plus drive in front of me, I hurried home to change.

"Maria, fancy seeing you here…"

I came through the door like a wet cat and looked up to see her tucked under a wool blanket, sipping on hot tea and scrolling through old movies.

"Yeah, stay away…"

"Ugh, sic?"

"Something is up, tried to hold it together, but by the sixth run to the bathroom, Cap sent me home."

I made a cross sign and held it up.

"I'll pick up some Lysol on my way home…"

I kicked off my shoes and stripped off my sweatshirt, tossing it in the washer on my way up the stairs.

"Headed to your mom's?"

"You guessed it…"

I brushed the rain from my hair, threw a light coat of makeup on my face, added some lipstick (as if it made a difference) and changed into a wool black sweater and a pair of blue jeans. I finished the look off with a pair of silver earrings and padded back down the stairs, perching on the sofa to put my socks on.

"You will never guess what I found out…"

I relayed the afternoon's events to Maria.

"Wow, that's some coincidence…"

"Yes, Richard thinks otherwise."

Maria looked at me. "Can you blame him?"

I shrugged and went for my shoes.

"Leave it to you. I like to think more rationally before projecting anything on my own life."

Maria read my thoughts. "I'll see if I can get any information on the case through the grapevine, know a few people I may be able to call."

"Thanks. I'll call you on my way back and see if you need anything."

"Thanks."

## Chapter 8

The drive out to the valley was usually a feast for the eyes, rolling hills of scented lush pines and blue-capped mountains; buildings and cities melted away to small towns and acres of farmland. Today, it was a slushy, wet mess, and what had started as a soft rain was now a torrent, sheets that melted against my windshield and made it hard to see. I slipped to the far right lane of the freeway and pulled off the Highline exit onto the back road. The two-lane highway slipped through the foothills and past the town of Preston and spilled into Fall City, nestled along the river front. It was a strip of shops and restaurants and a couple hundred houses. Everything that I was belonged to this place. It didn't matter if it had been a week or a month; so many memories found me every time. I pulled off the main road. As the rain let up and a bit of sun streaked through, I squinted, nearly blind in the sudden light, but it didn't matter. I knew the three rights and one left it took to reach Thirty-Third Street and the small two-story house. My brother's minivan was already parked in the drive behind my father's truck, and Aunt Carroll's was behind my mother's car, politely leaving me the street.

"What is this, a reunion?"

I headed across the front yard and up the porch steps, letting myself into the front room; the warmth and light of this place greeted me almost like a sudden assault. Aunt Carrol had left the house eventually when Julia was about two and moved into a small apartment across town. She worked hard to put herself through school and managed a nearby beauty salon but had never married or had any more children. I offered her a warm hug. It had been a few months since I had seen her.

"You look good, Aunty."

She touched my long hair and motherly kissed my forehead.

"Good to see you, kiddo. Wish Jewels could come, but she promised to be home for Christmas."

At twenty, Julia was in her first year of college in Spokane just a couple hours away. Besides myself, she had been the only one to leave this small town. Danny, my brother, sat in an armchair, rocking a baby no more than eight months old, who drifted sleepily in his father's arms. Danny had followed our dad, managing the small grocery store our father owned and operated and had married his girlfriend, Kate, two years out of high school. She had cashiered for a while until they had their first child, who was now a bubbling, bright ten-year-old girl who reminded her of herself at that age. In between her and the baby were two more gregarious boys, one six and one four; their hands and hearts were full.

"Hey, guys…"

I crouched to ruffle Chase and Mason's hair where they sat sprawled in front of cartoons.

"Danny…"

I kissed my brother's cheek and stroked the babies.

"Last one this time?"

I smirked at Kate, and the three shared a gentle laugh.

"Dad…"

He hugged me quickly. "How's life, kiddo?"

I shrugged. "Ya know…"

I followed the warm, fragrant scents to the kitchen where my mom sat humming and chopping celery. My family was not always picture perfect as they seemed to be that afternoon, but I was grateful I had them. I had grown up pretty blessed; I couldn't complain much.

"Can I help, Mom…?"

Without a word, she shoved some veggies my way and a knife. Looking up, our eyes met.

"Tell me what's new…?"

I longed to tell her all the things buried in my heart but kept the dialogue short and sweet, and she stuck to the usual mother hassle, which always ended up in the middle of my love life.

"Can you go out to the deep freeze and grab a loaf of bread, love?"

"Sure, Mom…"

I headed for the back porch, a small stoop covered by the roof creating the perfect dry place for a large deep freeze. As I popped open the lid and rummaged around for a large loaf of sourdough, when I stood back up and shut the lid, my gaze drifted across the fence line to the yellow house one row down. Shortly after Chris had left for college, the house had gone up for rent and his parents had moved away to Arizona mumbling away the usual convo of retirement, old age, and heat. The house had been rented twice, both families with young children.

"Who's in the yellow house, Mom?"

I brought the loaf back to the kitchen, unwrapped it, and set it to defrost in the microwave.

"It's been for sale for about a year. It pended for a while but then went back up for sale. Thinking of buying something closer to home?"

She smirked at me, and I brought the bread back to the butcher block where she was chopping veggies and sliced it in half, rummaging around the kitchen for butter and garlic.

"Ha ha, Mom, very funny."

The evening went as planned, the dining room table crowded as usual, kids running loose, babies crying, loudness and chaos, the usual beat. I was grateful for all of them but was even more grateful when goodbyes were said and I was headed back to my home to quiet and peace and solitude. The rain had gone and the clouds had parted, and it was a particularly dry evening. Stars glinted through wisps of clouds, and the air was chilly enough I could see my breath.

"Hey, Maria, can I stop and get you anything…?"

She answered groggily on the sixth ring and mumbled something about ginger ale and crackers.

"I'll see you in a bit."

I hung up and pulled into the Quick Stop 'n' shop in Preston before I hit the highway and headed down, my coat pulled tight against my wool sweater. I hurried inside away from the cold, leaving me no time to see the man coming out, and barreled headlong into him instead. Before I could topple onto the curb, two strong hands gripped my arms and held me upright.

"Oh God, I'm so sorry…"

I pulled back and looked up and felt every muscle in my entire body go loose. Every word faded from my mind. I never knew someone could be rendered speechless until that moment. His deep hazel eyes were looking back at me. A slow, curved smile came across his handsome face, and damn, had he not changed a bit.

"Chris?"

I stumbled back out of his arms and began to imagine I had gotten in a car accident and was lying in a coma in some hospital and this was a drug-induced dream, but the cold whipped around me and I knew I was very much awake.

"Michael?"

His grin widened, but I knew he was just as shocked to see me as I was to see him. I had never in a million years dreamed of ever seeing this man again, so seeing him there really standing before me, I was at a loss for what to say.

"I'll come back inside. You must be freezing…"

I followed him back through the doors, the bell clanging behind us, and thankfully, he broke the silence.

"God, I can't believe it's really you."

I felt his gaze roam across my body and shock, and Joy turned slightly to anger.

"What are you doing here, Chris?"

I walked off down the aisle in search of crackers. He followed behind. The familiar sound of his boots echoed in my heart. As a young woman, I had always imagined how the scene would play out if he ever graced my presence again, but now, standing here in the reality of it, I had nothing left to be angry at him for. We were kids then, and we had done the best we could.

"You mean back in town?"

Same old wit—some things never change. I scooped up a box of crackers and went to the cooler for a couple bottles of ginger ale and a Coke for myself for the remainder of the drive. Chicken soup and bread had induced the sleepies, carb overload.

"Ha ha, very funny."

Chris surveyed my loot.

"I came to check on the house. My parents are finally selling it. They didn't want to travel this time, asked me to meet with the real estate agent and assess things..." He paused and then added, "I'm here for about ten days, staying at a motel nearby..."

He trailed off but I felt such an onslaught of emotions I didn't know how to answer nor did I feel like he deserved an answer after all these years. I motioned to the items in my hand. "Sick roommate. I better get these home to her..."

I looked at him—almost studied him, rather—wondering what you say to the person you last saw when you were sixteen years old and madly in love with for the first time, who broke your heart and left you in emotional ruin. Maybe that's why I kept Richard close—because it had been too close to home, and then I just wanted to slap myself. *Girl, you're thirty years old. That was a lifetime ago—get your shit together.* I also wondered how in the world, after all the time that had transpired between us, this man could still leave me so undone.

"Yeah, sorry I'm keeping you, but really, it was good to see you, Michael."

I never left. I kept thinking, *You left. I couldn't find you, but you could have found me.*

*Wow*, I wondered aloud in my head. Maybe I needed a damn therapist of my own. I smiled instead and thought of all we had built together as friends long before the final blow.

"It's good to see you too, Chris."

He tucked his hands in his pockets and rocked on his heels, a nervous little gesture I knew from so long ago. "If you feel like catching up while I'm in town, that would be great."

I juggled the containers in my hands. For all I knew, he was married with kids or had turned into some low-life scumbag. God only knew, and honestly, I felt a little damn curious. "Sure, um..."

I looked down, not able to get to my phone. Chris took the hint and followed me to the register. I checked out and swung the bag near my hip. I felt his strong, steady gaze piercing through me as he opened the door and the cold night engulfed us again.

"Okay, go ahead."

I pulled out my phone, doing the "I will call you" game.

"Yeah, sure…"

Chris rattled off his number as I typed it in. I shivered a bit dramatically.

"I should let you get warm, so maybe I'll see you again?"

I offered him a slow smile.

"Maybe…"

I couldn't help but watch him walk off in those long, slow, familiar strides and climb in a small blue rented Ford Focus. I got in my car and turned up the heat, popping open the Coke bottle and heading for the freeway. If this day couldn't get any stranger, it just had. The dream from the other day, the memories all came back to me as I drove away and headed for the highway and home. They say there is a reason for everything.

## Chapter 9

Maria was half awake, half asleep when I came through the door a little over an hour ago and groggily reached for the ginger ale.

"You're a lifesaver."

I threw the crackers her way and peeled off my layers.

"You should be in bed resting," I commented as she sat upright, set the TV on mute, and began to sip the ginger ale.

"I finally quit puking two hours ago, so maybe I'll get there soon."

I scrunched up my face and kicked off my shoes, my mind restless I headed for the kitchen to make some tea. "Thanks for that."

Maria giggled softly and continued to sip the soda. "How was your night anyways?"

I set the tea kettle to boil and set a bag of chamomile in a cup. "Interesting. Not sure if you have the strength to launch into a full convo right now."

She made a scoffing noise. "I'll let you sit on the other side of the room."

I fixed my tea and took the armchair several feet from her, knowing it was all ridiculous, since we breathed the same air. "Well, everything went well at my mom's. The usual, you know—she said to tell you hi and you're welcome anytime."

Maria munched tentatively on a cracker. "Your eyes speak volumes, girl."

I sighed and hugged my cup, sipping and letting the warmth hit my chilled bones.

"Okay, if you insist. I ran into an old friend…Chris, actually. He's there to sell his parents' house, I guess…"

Maria cut me off.

"Who—wait, *the* Chris?"

Even though she had never met the guy and the period he had been so prominent in my life had come and gone before we had met, I realized she still knew way more than she possibly should about this man.

"Yes, *the* Chris."

I sipped more tea, and we proceeded to chat on about the strangeness of the evening and my mixed emotions until sleep finally caught up to her and I sent her off to bed.

# Chapter 10

"Mrs. Black?"

I looked up from my desk to see a man standing in my doorway. Debra had rung my line in the middle of a less than promising lunch of a takeout roast beef on rye.

"Yes, come in. Detective, sit wherever you like." I motioned to the sitting area and tossed the remaining half a sandwich in the trash.

"Sorry to interrupt your lunch, ma'am, but I have some questions I need to ask you…"

He was tall, and he fit awkwardly in the arm chair, dressed in a dark gray suit and matching tie. I guessed him old enough to be seasoned in his line of business. No sooner had Debra flipped the open sign on the door, the detective called, suggesting he would drop by. The morning had faded away to noon before he had made his arrival.

"It's no problem. I'm happy to help."

"You were Mr. Jefferson's therapist, correct?"

"Yes, for about a year, but that was eight months ago. I haven't seen him for any more sessions."

The detective busied himself by scrawling notes. "So you haven't seen him for eight months then?"

"That's correct…"

"What were you seeing Mr. Jefferson for?"

I crossed my arms about my chest, knowing even though he was dead—murdered at that—I had to keep this as discreet as possible.

"Mild depression, some anxiety. After about twelve months' worth of sessions, he called it quits."

"Any reason for his sudden departure?"

I let my arms go, fiddling with something on my desk I felt the detective's eyes narrowing in on me, and I felt even more nervous. God help me—I hadn't done anything wrong, but he was still making me nervous as hell.

"No, he just came in one day said that it would be his last session, felt I had helped him tremendously. My recommendation was that it might benefit him to continue seeing me, but I couldn't stop him from leaving either."

I braced myself for it, realizing I had thrown myself to the lions.

"Did you feel there was a reason he would benefit from further therapy?"

"It was just my suggestion, Detective. I felt there were still some stressors he could work on that were causing his anxiety, but never once did I feel it was anything serious."

The detective took another ten or fifteen minutes of my time, and we danced around the same issue, asked what seemed the same questions in different ways as if he were looking for something to pop up. I suppose that was his job.

"Well, thank you for your time, Miss Black. If you think of anything further, please give me a call."

He handed me his card, and I saw him to the door. No sooner had he left than my personal cell began ringing.

"Make it quick, Richard, I got a client in five minutes," I nearly snapped, picking up the phone.

"Well, hello to you too…"

I sighed and sat down. "Sorry, I feel like I have just been given the third degree."

"I know the feeling."

That he did.

"Anyways, just some general questions. He didn't ask me about you. It's not like we were married and left a paperwork trail. I'm sure nothing will come up. Your good reputation will not be tarnished."

I heard him laugh softly. "Very funny…"

I heard Debra buzz in on the other line. "Listen, I gotta go, but if he asks me anything, I'll answer him truthfully, but there is no reason for me to say anything nor is there for you."

I hung up and went about my business for the rest of the afternoon till all the lamps were burning in the small office and Debra was standing at my door. I stopped in the middle of writing down some daily notes.

"You can go home, Debra. I have some things to finish. I'll lock up…"

"Evening clients?"

I always let Debra work her nine-to-five and flew solo after that for sometimes a remaining two hours for working clients. Today, I thankfully didn't have anything on the schedule, and if my good fortune fell on a Monday or a Friday, I was always extra thankful.

"Thankfully not. Enjoy your evening. Say hi to your hubby for me."

"Will do. Night."

I turned back to the papers at hand and finished writing out some notes for the day and logging some numbers for my accountant. I didn't hear the bell ring twice. I simply heard the rattle once and assumed it was Debra leaving.

"Fuck!" I took in a sharp breath, dropping the pen in my hand. My heart started to hammer in my chest, and I reached for the phone out of pure instinct.

"Don't even try it."

The pistol came in my face so fast I didn't have time to blink. My life felt as if it were flashing in front of me as fear swelled in me. I tried desperately to remain calm. Between the voice and the build, I knew it was a man standing before me—the black sweater, gloves, pants, and ski mask left the rest to imagination.

"What do you want? If it's drugs, I'm not a doctor. I don't carry a prescription pad or anything on—"

His fist was hot and hard and threw fire that exploded against my cheekbone, knocking me back in my chair.

"Shut up and listen!"

I sat upright, feeling my cheek swell almost instantly. I threw my hands up in surrender.

"Give me James Jefferson's file now!"

"Okay, it's in my briefcase…"

I motioned behind me to the floor; he swung around the desk and held the gun over my head.

"Don't try anything funny."

I bent over and pulled the file out and slowly held it out. The armed man snatched it from me and backed up to the door before disappearing. I sat frozen and motionless for a long second before I finally let out the breath I had been holding. I felt my cheek and winced then finally reached for the phone but stopped. What the hell was I going to tell the cops? That some masked intruder came in and stole a deceased patient's file, and oh, I'm sure it has something to do with your investigation but I couldn't identify him if I tried? As my heart pounded back to normal, I knew it was time to head home.

* * *

"What happened to you?"

I didn't break into tears until I was through my front door and Maria was on me with an icepack like a ninja.

"Do I need to beat some guy up?"

I sank down to the sofa, wincing as I laughed and wiping tears from my eyes. "Thanks."

I felt new pain stab up my cheek as I placed the icepack on the throbbing lump, wondering how in the world even with good makeup I would explain that one to my patients tomorrow. I suppose that was the least of my worries at the moment.

"No, I'm fine, I think..."

Maria sat next to me and examined my cheek. "By that bruise I would say not."

I sat back against the sofa and felt a new wave of tears come over me but pushed them aside it was just the rush of the fear subsiding. "Some guy came into my office after Debra left and took the file at gunpoint..."

"Jesus, Micky, why didn't you call the cops? Thank God you're all right...and file—what do you mean *file*?"

She looked at me funny and got up splashing some rum into two cups. She came back over and handed me one. I let the liquor burn warmly down my throat and into my stomach, calming my nerves slowly.

"Jefferson, Mr. James Jefferson. I read over that file, Maria, there was nothing in it…"

"Apparently there was, still think you—"

I set the cup and the ice down.

"And tell them what? He stole some paper?"

"On a victim whose murder they're investigating? Micky, use your head on this."

I stood up suddenly. "I need a shower and to change and clear my head."

I headed upstairs and glanced in the mirror over my dresser, touched the lump that would swell into an obvious bruise by morning light, and stripped out of my skirt and blouse quickly. I ran the shower as hot as I could stand and stood under the firm spray, relishing how it massaged my skin and seemed to release the tension out of my day. I stayed in long enough to rinse off and wash my hair before climbing out and stepping into a pair of black yoga pants and white T-shirt. I pulled on a fresh pair of socks, used the towel to wring some more water out of my hair, and flopped down on the bed. I wondered idly if I should even tell the cops what had transpired, but mostly, my curiosity burned the hardest. I had been over that file back to front. I had conjured up every memory I could think of. James Jefferson was, at the end of the day, just like any other patient of mine. I got up after a long moment listening to Maria moving downstairs probably making dinner and was thankful on a night like tonight that I did not live alone. I padded over to my dresser again and opened a music box that I had been gifted from my grandmother as a little girl; it sat atop a small box with a single drawer, large enough to house three letters. Needing a distraction, I had been thinking about them since Saturday and figured know was as good a time as any to read them again. Chris's twenty-year-old self spoke to me in three short letters and then drifted from my life completely. Why I still had them I did not know. I hadn't looked at them in so long I had almost forgotten they were there. I put them back and reached for my phone, scrawled through my numbers, and paused on his. The thought of calling him seemed so odd yet so comforting in that moment.

"Micky, you okay up there?" I heard Maria call, as smells of tomato sauce and spices drifted up from the kitchen.

"Yeah, just a second." I set my phone back and headed downstairs. Maria was boiling pasta on the stove and heating a jar of tomato sauce at the same time.

"Mmmmm, my fave smells great."

She smiled back. "Ah, what are friends for?"

We were quiet for a while, breaking bread and digging into pasta and salad till Maria finally spoke.

"I found some things out today, but after your debacle, I'm not sure you wanted to hear it."

I poured a second glass of wine, not quite tipsy but definitely feeling it. I reached for another piece of bread.

"Let me guess whom it's about..."

Maria's fork clattered on her plate.

"Not much more than the basics..."

I looked at her as I chewed bread.

"I'm okay, really. I want to hear..."

Maria took a sip from her own glass.

"One shot to the back of the head, execution-style, looks like he had been bound up first. Rope marks were found on his wrists and ankles but no rope."

"Geezus, so he was taken there unwillingly and no witnesses?"

"Time of death was several hours prior, probably had been dumped sometime late morning when it was still dark, probably used a silencer, I'm guessing. One weird thing was a red silk tie used to gag him."

I shook my head.

"Definitely some personal motive there, intimate almost—someone who knew him really well. Was he wearing a suit?"

Maria shook her head.

"Sweatshirt and jeans."

"So it was brought with them, whoever committed the crime. Yes, definitely a crime of passion."

Maria pondered this for a moment.

"Anyone you know who might have a personal vendetta against him?"

I shook my head. "He had his faults, but I don't know why anyone would want him dead."

"Money. Check this—he was worth like three million, did pretty damn well in real estate."

I whistled. "Nice chunk of change for sure."

Maria got up and collected plates despite my protest. "He was an easy target, Micky. Guy like that walking around with all that money…"

I took the remaining wine to the living room. "He definitely liked to be flashy. So you just think this was some high-speed robbery?"

Maria joined me.

"I did, but after what happened tonight, I'm not so sure."

"I know. It's almost like someone is trying to hide something. What, I don't know."

# Chapter 11

"That's it!"

The girl grabbed the file hastily and rummaged through the single sheets of paper, looking for something anything she could sink her teeth into, but nothing transpired. Her thin blond hair ruffled around her heart-shaped face as her pink lips drew back against perfect white teeth. Her eyes looked up to the man standing before her. She was all of five feet, three inches and a hundred and twenty-seven pounds. This man before her outdid her by twice that, but she showed no fear.

"I can't believe this… I can't believe how much I paid you and this is the dirt you dig up? A pathetic intake file from his therapist? I thought you were smarter than that!"

The girl raised the handgun and aimed it at the man's head. He threw his hands up. He was well over six feet and could have taken her in an instant. Instead, he stood frozen in front of her in surrender.

"Katie, please, we can work this out. I…"

Her hands tightened around the gun. Carl was as disposable as they come. He had successfully taken James out of the picture for her for nothing more than a small sum of cash. Katie knew he was a useless witness to her, and she didn't even let him finish the sentence. She fired once and he fell almost instantly to the cold, hard pavement. The girl pocketed the gun. Satisfied, the thumping music from the tavern had drowned out all noise, she turned to leave, and then she smirked and peered down at the name of the therapist. Another woman in James's life. She took the paper out and tossed the file down near the body with the bold letters of "Property of Black Therapy Group" stamped on front.

"Try that on for size!"

She turned and headed back to her car, a little dark-blue Honda. She backed up and sped out of the alley, her mind turning a million miles a minute as she raced down the wet, dark streets of Seattle. Katie sighed a huge sigh of relief as she merged onto I5 and headed out of the city. 'Twas only one last thing to do before her plan was complete and hoping with this new turn of events, Michael would stay out of her way.

# Chapter 12

I did the best to brush makeup over the purplish-blue mark high on my cheekbone and dressed in a silk maroon blouse and charcoal-gray slacks. I tossed my stuff together and headed downstairs for a quick cup of coffee before I headed out to the office.

"Be careful. Call me later. Love ya."

Maria had stuck a Post-It to the coffee maker, half a pot still plenty warm. I fished a travel cup out of the cupboard. I had never had a sister, but if I had to pick one for myself, she would be it. I filled the cup, splashed in some creamer, and headed to my car. I wondered idly if yesterday was the end of my transaction with the stranger. Needing a distraction, I dialed the one number I had almost thought of erasing from my phone as I drove into work.

"Hey, you've reached Chris. Leave a message…"

At eighty-thirty in the morning, a man on a semi vacation I should have figured he wouldn't be up at this hour.

"Hey, it's me. Michael, call me when you get a chance. Thought maybe we could meet tonight if you're free."

No sooner had I clicked the hang-up button and pulled into a steady line of traffic did the phone buzz again. I pushed the talk switch, and his familiar voice filled the cab of the car once again.

"Hey, sorry I was in the shower. Um…"

It was ridiculous how two adults could suddenly become like awkward teenagers in a matter of minutes.

"I'm driving into work. Thought I would see what you were up to. If you're willing to drive, I'll meet you?"

"Yeah, sure. What time were you thinking?"

"Seven, give or take traffic. I'll meet you halfway. I know a great Thai place in Bellevue."

"Seven is great—send me the name I'll throw it in my GPS."

I paused, wondering if I should say something else, but I was at a loss for words.

"Okay, sounds good. So I'll see you tonight?"

"Yep."

We hung up, and I smacked my hand on my forehead, congratulating myself for the world's most awkward phone call. The day went as smoothly as one could expect when your therapist shows up with a shiner. The few newer clients of mine, I did a little less explaining to, and to the ones who had been seeking therapy from me for a while, I explained as best I could. For the most part, it was relatively less than half of the people I saw that day. I was able to close up shop on time but not able to make it through traffic in time. He got there before I did and took the liberty of ordering for both of us. I didn't think I was a bit hungry until I smelled the fragrant white rice and bowls of yellow curry.

"Hope you don't mind, I was starving."

I pulled out my chair and sat down with a heavy sigh, brushing my long black locks back from my face. I felt his gaze on me.

"What happened to your cheek?"

I thought of the first thing that popped in my head, and unfortunately, as a mental health professional, I knew it was the oldest line in the book.

"Nothing…fell down some stairs…"

Chris wasn't one to look past my lies. I pointed a fork at him.

"I'm not married, no current boyfriend, nothing like that, I promise. Just don't worry about it, okay? How about you tell me about you?"

I took a bite of rice and chicken, savoring the sweet and spice.

"No, never married, no kids, got kinda close, I guess. I was engaged to a girl. We were together almost four years, broke up about a year ago."

We fell back into old ways. It was so easy to feel comfortable around him after all these years, and that was mighty dangerous in ways I couldn't afford right know.

"God, it's good to see you again. I wasn't sure how this would go if…if I ever saw you again."

His eyes caught mine, and the waitress came over to clear our plates. He reached for my hand, but I pulled away.

"Michael, I meant to—I don't know. I thought about you a lot at first after those last letters I wrote, but I loved you so much in so many ways, but I…I didn't want to break your heart."

I looked at him. He didn't want to break a young girl's heart. What did he think dropping off the face of the earth would do? For a second, I was that fiery young sixteen-year-old who wanted to give him a piece of my mind, and then I realized it was simply foolish.

"We were both kids. It's okay." I snatched the check before he could make a grab for it. "On me. No arguments."

Chris held up his hands in surrender. I left a tip as well, and we gathered up our coats, heading into the chill of the night. A blanket of misty rain fell, deepening the chill.

"I got work in the morning. I should head home."

I shivered in my jacket, wanting to linger, to ask him for coffee, to continue into the night, to forget I was an adult with no responsibilities.

"Of course. Thanks for dinner…"

Chris awkwardly walked me to my car and held open the door.

"Get in before you freeze."

I wanted to hug him with sudden intensity just to see how it felt. I climbed in the car instead and flipped over the engine, getting the heat going.

"When do you head home?"

"I fly out late Sunday. Can I call you?"

I smiled.

"Yeah, that would be nice…"

I watched him saunter away again and shook my head. Sighing and leaning back in my seat, I let the heat warm me and watched his car pull away before I headed out myself. How in the world had this crazy boy so recklessly fallen back into my life? I wanted our friendship back but was embarrassed to say I wanted a little more back, a little more we had never had. I let my mind wander down memory lane as I drove home through the rain.

"Mmmm, Michael…"

His hand was on my face, his lips close to mine. I felt my heart rush inside my chest. I giggled and lay back; the stuffed unicorns stared at me on the white four poster bed from their perch on my matching dresser.

"My father would kill me if he knew you were here while he was out, let alone in this room."

Chris chuckled and lay beside me, making my heart flutter harder.

"But he's not here. No one's here…"

I felt his mouth on me again—the taste of him, the smell of him. I let his hand glide up under my T-shirt and slide across the top of my bra.

"Mmmm, cowboy, slow down…"

I turned on my side facing him.

"Baby, I love you…"

I smiled wide. I had waited almost the entire year to hear those words, and now here, with him leaving on a college scholarship that was sending him all the way to California; he whispered it affectionately in my ear.

"I love you too, cowboy…"

His mouth found mine again, and this time, when his hand slipped up my, tee I let him unhook my bra strap. I sighed and shivered in his arms as I felt his hands touch my bare skin, and suddenly, I wanted all of him in a way I had never wanted anyone else and not because of those words but because I felt loved in my heart, protected and trusted by this man.

"Michael!"

My mother's voice followed her bang through the front door, and I'm not sure which of us jumped off the bed faster.

"She is gonna kill us both but mostly you…"

We scrambled to right our clothes, and I shoved him out the door as fast as I could.

"Hey, Mom, we were just hanging out in the yard…"

She dropped her keys and purse on the kitchen counter and eyeballed both of us.

"Mmmmm hmmm, we'll talk later. Chris, I think you're wanted home."

Chris pecked my cheek.

"I'll call you later, Mrs. Black."

"Mom, why do you have to be like that?"

I began pulling groceries out of bags and putting things away. My mom went about prepping for dinner, and for a moment that seemed to stretch into eternity, we didn't talk.

"You're sixteen, he's nineteen. Maybe that doesn't mean much in five or six years, darling, but it means a lot right now, and the only reason we let you two date is you have been friends for a long time and I know him well enough to know he would never disrespect you."

My mom pointed a zucchini accusingly at me and then began chopping in a vicious rhythm.

"Well, he is leaving tomorrow, so you won't have to worry about it anymore!" I snapped, slamming the last box of cereal in the pantry and turning to leave.

"Michael…"

My mother turned around and grabbed my arm, tugging me back toward her. "I love you. I want what's best for you. I think staying friends is reasonable, but I think you're treading in water that's too deep…"

I took my arm back and wrapped my arms around myself. "You and Dad married out of high school."

My mother sighed. "Because I was…I loved your father very much and maybe I would have married him anyways, but—"

"Yeah, yeah, yeah. I've heard this story a thousand times. Because you got pregnant with Danny. Well, I'm not that stupid, Mom!"

I regretted the words as soon as they flew out of my mouth, looking like I had thrown daggers at my mother, but in my sixteen-year-old heart in love for the very first time, I was blind to everything else. All I wanted was Chris, and I couldn't imagine him wanting anything else.

"I'm going to pretend I didn't hear that, Michael. Love is fragile at your age, and Chris has a great opportunity, and I hope to see you get there one day."

I stormed out of the kitchen and slammed my bedroom door. Collapsing on my bed, I punched at the pillows.

God, we tried. How we tried for six whole months—a few letters, a half a dozen or so phone calls, but it just didn't work. Maybe it could have, but he pulled away from me, and then I blamed him for every ounce of pain my heart went through, but now, looking back, having gone through my twenties myself, I realized I had been asking a lot of a situation that was doomed to fail.

Maria thankfully wasn't home when I came through the door soaking wet from the rain. I dropped my things by the door and headed straight for the shower. As soon as heat had soaked back into my bones and I was in a dry pair of clothes, my wet hair brushed back my face without makeup and the most comfy set of yoga pants I could find. I poured a tall glass of wine, flicked the fireplace on, and fired up the laptop. Opening up my electronic notes on Mr. Jefferson, I was bound to get to the bottom of this.

"Show me what you're hiding…" I sipped my wine and murmured to the electronic screen as if whatever had led to James's demise would pop up and bite me. After all the events that had transpired, I had a feeling it wasn't all that simple. I worked through my electronic notes, depression scales I had taken on James, and any memories of the man who had graced my office weekly for nearly a year. She came to me like a sudden assault, and I paused as I read over the notes and realized her name had appeared shortly into our sessions and stayed for quite a while before he refused to discuss it anymore. A girl named Katie. What stuck out the most was the fact he said there relationship had ended on a sour note. He had been forced to file a restraining order on her. She was also the only girl he mentioned (out of many) that he had called by a first name. Even though it stuck out like a sore thumb now, I wondered why I hadn't see it before. For a glamorous moment, it was hard to imagine that someone, let alone a woman, could cause such a heinous crime, and how could something go from a mild restraining order to full-blown rage and murder? Although it didn't fit the typical profile, working in the mental health field, I knew anything was possible.

Just as my thoughts began to form and turn into a runaway train, a sudden loud banging on my front door made me nearly jump out of my skin. I clutched the material of my shirt close to my heart and crept slowly to the front door, my eyes surveying the room for a weapon, when I realized it was foolish to think that the perp would come knocking on my door—that would be too convenient.

"Detective Langley?"

I swung open the door to find the detective that had been in my office the week prior standing on my doorstep at nine at night on a Saturday. I knew that could only mean one thing.

"Miss Black, I would like you to come down to the police department for some questioning."

I balked. Now what the hell was going on? "Can I ask what this is about?"

"The recent murder of James Jefferson now if—"

I cut him off. "Whatever questions you have to ask me, you can ask me inside."

"I'm afraid not, ma'am. Please come with me—you can make this easy or hard."

The detective's hand lightly touched his side, where I knew his gun was holstered.

"Can you give me a moment?" I swung the door wide so he could step inside and grabbed my jacket and shoes, feeling more like a suspect as he led me to the back of the patrol car.

"Excuse me, but is this necessary?"

"You're being detained for investigation into the murder of James Jefferson."

"So I am a suspect? Aren't you supposed to read me my rights or something?"

The detective smirked at my wit. "You're not being charged... yet."

He let the last word linger. It was a long drive into the station. As the rain pounded on the roof of the sedan, a thousand thoughts flew through my head. This was the last thing I had expected running my own practice, but I couldn't be in my clients life, and all situations were plausible, I suppose.

I felt like I was in an episode of *Law and Order*. The detective led me back to a small room with slate-gray walls. The furniture wasn't any more welcoming, just a small metal table and matching chairs, supposing the company that occupied this place simply was best.

"I would like to take your prints if I can, Miss Black."

Another officer stepped into the room.

"And if I say no?"

I looked at him and nodded.

"Yeah, yeah, I get it—easy or hard."

Great—a therapist building her reputation now had her fingerprints on file with the SPD.

"Now can you tell me what all this is about please?"

The detective took the chair opposite me and placed a manila file folder on the table in a plastic bag. I recognized James's name and my own cursive writing immediately.

"Where did you get that?"

"I think that's a question you need to answer, Miss Black."

I looked at him as if this was some joke.

"Are you kidding me?"

He suddenly pointed to my cheek.

"That's quite the shiner you have there—looks pretty recent."

No way come hell or high water was this man going to place me in the vicinity of this man's murder.

"We have another victim, Miss Black. He has yet to be identified—found about an hour ago in an alley, single gunshot wound to the head, a lot like Mr. Jefferson, but more curiously, this was found on him and empty as well."

He leaned forward into my space almost intimidatingly.

"Care to explain?"

I realized I had nowhere else to go.

"It was stolen."

The detective looked at me quizzically almost to see if I was bluffing.

"If it was stolen, why didn't you report it?"

I chuckled. "Say what, Detective? That some masked guy came into my office and stole some paper?"

"Apparently it was more than just paper, Miss Black. My best guess is there was something someone wanted…or maybe you wanted to get someone out of the way?"

The Detective threw it back in my court, so I doubled down. "Listen, unless you have something to charge me with, I believe I'm free to go."

"Your fingerprints are all over this file, Miss Black. That links you to the crime at hand. In fact, I can charge you with murder."

I threw my hands out. "Then charge me, else we are done here."

"Do you have any surveillance cameras anything that corroborates the story of this masked gunman…" He drew out the words slowly as if I was lying through my teeth, infuriating me further.

"I have no reason to." I pointed to my cheek. "Only this."

"What about the hours prior to this?"

I grumbled, realizing I had mostly been alone up until the detective had showed up at my door.

"Let me guess—you were home alone?"

"I can only vouch for my time period up until 5:00 p.m. when my assistant, Debra, left the office."

The detective stood up. "Would you be willing to take a polygraph?"

I eyed him as if I had a choice. "Sure, whatever you need, Detective."

I left within the hour, refusing a ride from the police officer. I called for a taxi. The rain had let up, but the cold pressed down on me as I climbed in the cab of the car and headed home. I wondered about this Katie person who had seemed to have a lot of meaning in his life. Was she out there somewhere? Did she have a hand in the end of James's life? I couldn't imagine a restraining order could lead to murder, but love can do some diabolical things. Maria was home by the time I made it back, and I was surprised to find her up at a quarter past eleven; she was in pj's, eating cereal and leaning against the counter. The TV flickered, mostly for sound and company.

"Well, where have you been?"

"I'm sorry I couldn't answer my phone. I got detained."

Maria set the bowl in the sink with a clatter.

"As in police detained?"

I sank down to the sofa with a heavy sigh. "Yes, they found another body. Let's just say I don't have to worry about him coming after me."

Maria joined me.

"How did they link you to—"

I cut her off. "The damn file folder he stole was empty in his hand. Someone took the papers for whatever it was worth and apparently worth a lot."

"Damn!"

I ran my hands through my hair.

"I took a lie detector test just to clear my name, and I'm pretty sure they know everything they need to know about me. I hope it doesn't have any negative repercussions when it comes down to you."

I looked at her suddenly, and she shrugged.

"I'll do what I can to help—"

I stood up suddenly.

"Unless they decide I'm a murderer…"

"They have no DNA evidence to link you."

I threw up my hands.

"I am though. I'm tied into this whether I like it or not. Now I just don't understand the importance of that file!"

"Maybe you need to let Richard know."

"As if he had anything to do with this."

"Maybe it's not what's in the file, it's the admission of a person…"

I looked at her suddenly.

"I was thinking the same thing. There is one girl in particular he referenced by name and even mentioned have a restraining order placed on her."

"Sounds like you have your answer. Listen, morning comes fast. I have to head to bed, stay out of trouble."

# Chapter 13

I ate toast and drank coffee over the morning news. It was less fruitful in putting to light who got killed last night. It was secondary information that read no more than a body found shot in an alley on Pioneer Square. Police were still investigating. It was funny when money and status was involved how abruptly things changed. Which led me back to Mr. Jefferson. I was never one to pry into my patients' personal lives, but I figured in this instance, it didn't matter, and police be damned, I was going to do a little investigating of my own before my name got dragged through the mud any more.

James's place of employment was a small firm he ran in Medina, a quiet neighborhood with lavish houses spread along Lake Washington connected to Seattle by the floating bridge. Those who could afford it worked in the downtown office buildings in Seattle and often commuted back to Medina. I grabbed my keys and headed out, making a quick call into my own office on the way.

"Debra, please reschedule my morning patients. Offer them a later evening appointment or see what I have open for the rest of the week…including the weekend if need be."

The rain had ceased, and puffy cottony white clouds floated in a blue sea. A cool wind reminded me October and winter were just around the corner as I pulled into the four slot parking lot in front of the one-story office building made to look like a quaint country home. Large magnolia trees framed large picture windows. An open sign hung on the frosted glass front door, and I let myself into a warm, inviting lobby, again creating the homey feel with a large tan sofa and matching armchairs, magazines spread across a glass coffee tables where candles scented the air with fragrances of vanilla.

"May I help you?"

A tall, attractive woman sat behind a white desk dressed up in a pair of slacks and a blouse, brown tresses pulled back from a soft round face and large hazelnut eyes, her smile tinted red. She stopped clattering her nails along the keyboard of the computer. I stepped forward, thinking carefully about my words.

"Mr. Jefferson was my real estate agent..."

Her mouth formed an *O*, and I took it they had been fielding a lot of clients over the last few weeks.

"Let me get Mr. Davis for you just a moment. I believe he's still in."

Two long legs headed down a short hall and disappeared around a corner. I heard knocking and voices, and then she returned to her perch.

"He'll be with you in a moment. He's on the phone."

I waited a good ten minutes in a nearby chair till Mr. Davis appeared, a well-built man next door—handsome and a good twenty years younger than the former Mr. Jefferson.

"Call me Tim. How may I help you, miss?"

I shook his hand.

"Michael."

"Come on back and let's see how we can help you out. It's been crazy busy as you can imagine around here..."

Tim sighed and led me into a cozy office; a small desk and two bookshelves faced a set of matching black chairs. I took a seat as he sat back down behind his desk.

"Poor James. Great man, great mentor."

"So I've heard."

Tim shuffled papers.

"Enough of that. Let me know what property you were interested in. James may have owned and operated this place, but he still hit the pavement frequently selling houses right along with the rest of us."

I stalled.

"So you're running the show."

Quick sad smile.

"More or less. James didn't have children."

"Well, it's a great honor I'm sure."

Tim nodded.

"Yes, but shall we get back to the matter at hand?"

I sighed and pressed forward, thinking the worst he could possibly do was kick me out on my butt.

"Listen, there wasn't a property. I was…I was James's therapist, and well—"

Tim stood up quickly.

"Listen, I don't know what you want to hear that the police haven't already asked me, Michael. If you're not here about a property, well then, I'm going to have to see you out."

I stood up as he pointed to the door, wondering why he was getting so defensive almost immediately. I held up my hands.

"Listen, it's a long story how I got involved, but anything you can tell me, that would be—"

Tim cut me off.

"Then feel free to ask the police. Now if you don't mind, I have some real clients to help…"

Tim emphasized the *we* pretty firmly, and I let myself out.

James's home address was listed as five miles away on the GPS, a few quick turns down thick tree-lined streets, unique two- and three-story houses, new and well-aged spread amply apart and some even gated or nearly invisible by long snaking drives. Soon I found myself in front of an older brick home sharply dressed in garden beds overflowing with foliage and fall mums. It was smaller than I had imagined a man of wealth like Mr. Jefferson owning. One single floor that looked around two thousand square feet with a two-car garage. It was a well-maintained classic. Two long-paned windows were closed tight by cream drapes, and an electric blue door stood half open against a glass screen pane. A silver Jaguar suggested someone was home. I parked across the street along a row of laurel bushes blocking out the front of the neighbors' houses and stepped out. I smoothed my charcoal blazer over my silk-colored champagne top. I had dressed a step up that morning. Black pumps blended well with my gray slacks.

The noise of my shoes and the rustle of my attire made my presence known well before I was halfway up the front walk.

"If you're interested in the property, you can get the hell back. I've told you people it's not for sale!"

The sharp voice belonged to a woman who appeared suddenly in the doorway—blue jeans and a white knit sweater and tennis shoes, her hair unkempt and tied back, her face without makeup. Anger flooded out of her.

"Ma'am, I'm not here to inquire about the property. I just had a few questions to ask you?"

I paused, asserting myself and hoping she took me seriously. The woman shifted the box she was carrying to her hip.

"What are you, the police? Show me some identification." The voice softened a bit, and the eyes roamed over me, half accusing, half questioning.

"No, I'm not the police either."

The laugh was shrill and pierced the air, sending a few birds squawking from the trees.

"Ha! I should have guessed it the first time—the way you're dressed, prancing your cute self in here—you're one of them, aren't you?"

Back to anger we went.

"Excuse me?"

"Listen, I came to clean my brother's house out a few days ago, and those tramps have been all up here, acting all sorrowful but mostly trying to get their greedy hands on whatever they can. My brother was a great guy, but women…women were his fault. He had too many relationships. If you ask me, he had this coming, probably finally did the right woman wrong!"

Brother? I felt surprised at that. James had never divulged he had siblings, let alone parents. He refused to talk about that or place it on his intake forms. For all I knew, the man was hatched from an egg.

"No, I promise I wasn't involved with your brother. Well, not like that. I…I was his therapist."

Her face cracked a smile. "Well, there's one you don't hear every day, my brother in therapy. So what the hell did you come all this way for?"

I stepped closer, testing the waters, and she fortunately stepped back and let the box go just inside the door.

"I saw a therapist once a couple years ago when I lost my husband. She was a pretty caring soul, but this seems to be…"

I stepped up on the front porch.

"A little unethical, I know, but the police have been asking me a ton of questions, and I'm just honestly trying to gather some answers of my own."

"You should know enough about him. You were his therapist."

The snap in her voice came back.

"Only what he cared to tell me, and apparently, that wasn't much."

She opened the door wider and sized me up again. I couldn't help but notice she was probably a good ten or fifteen years older than her brother.

"Let me guess—he never mentioned me at all or our parents."

I shook my head.

"I was just thinking about taking a break. Come in, I guess, though I don't know how much help I can be."

It felt weird as my heels clacked on the wood floors. The outside of the house was very different than the inside, which had a more modern taste and feel, and I could definitely see where some of James's small fortune had been planted. I followed her through the front room, walls washed in cool bluish steel gray and several paintings in lush florals, and Impressionist pieces lined them. The furniture was a soft, supple black leather, and the coffee table was a glass oval over a sculpted mermaid. What had once been the brick facade of an old fireplace was painted a shade of deep gray and was the backdrop of a lacquered bar and a couple of matching stools. I followed her through saloon doors into a kitchen made of granite and stainless steel, a dining room to the right, and a more modest-looking TV room to the left and a hallway I surmised led to the bedrooms.

"I'm Susan, by the way."

I shook her hand.

"Michael."

No curious eyebrow was raised, as she pulled a couple diet cokes out and handed me one.

"Four women have been by in the last couple days. Nearly had to call the police on a few. Maybe I should have let them have at the property. Nothin' I need in here."

She threw her hands up and stepped into the TV room and sat down on a coffee-brown sectional. The back windows looked across a large deck and a hot tub. There was no grass, just patio cement, perfect for entertaining. I popped open the Coke and joined her.

"I have never been here. The last time I saw my brother was ten years ago at my parents' funeral. Now theirs was a love story. Both in their eighties, he had a massive heart attack. She passed away three days later in her sleep. I spoke to my brother maybe twice a year, sent a Christmas card. That was the type of relationship we had. Wasn't either one of our faults I guess. I was fourteen when he was born. Both my parents were business smart—both into real estate, owned their own company as well, turned quite a profit, but didn't have much time for anything else. I mean they loved me very much, doted on me, but James, he wasn't in the cards. He happened in my mother's forties. The story has been told a million times I'm sure…"

Susan paused and sipped the Coke. Her eyes roamed the room for a moment as if lost in thought.

"Anyways, he was the baby. He was spoiled, never really disciplined. I always remember him getting away with everything and getting everything he wanted. I was always the one they expected everything from, sent me to a good college, expected good grades, all of that. I did just that—graduated from law school actually—eventually married. I have a couple teenagers of my own back in California…"

"What led James here?"

Susan sighed.

"Real estate market, I suppose. We were from a small town in California. I'm sure you might know that part. I went into the city to attend UCLA and then settled in Pasadena. After that, I never really had a desire to leave other than travel, of course, at times, but James—he left as soon as he could, traveled quite a bit, never really talked to him but always heard it from my mother."

Susan rolled the silver can between her hands. The large diamond glinted against her wedding band. I wondered if the family held considerable wealth all the way around that perhaps money had been the motive.

"I'm sorry for your loss."

Susan shrugged.

"I never wished him any harm, but the truth was we were too far apart in age and we never had anything in common. James was always a party boy. You could say I went off to have a career, knowing all along that I would get married and have children. That was a desire he never had. I never really got to know him—that's the sad part—and now he's gone."

Susan got up suddenly, crossed the room, and touched a couple of picture frames idly. I thought I noticed tears.

"I don't need any of this. Charity is picking up the furniture. The house will go on the market next week. It's all willed to me. Probably dump that money into a couple other children's charities I help run back home. Can I ask you a question?"

Susan turned, padded back over, and sat down and really looked at me. All of this made me feel slightly uncomfortable.

"Why you? Why therapy? Sorry, no offense, but James always seemed to have his shit together. Then again, what do I know?"

I sighed and treaded lightly not wanting to divulge too much information but trying to be as open and candid as she had been with me.

"He wasn't hiding anything if that's what you're wondering, just stressed. Seemed a little anxious and depressed."

Susan chuckled.

"Why am I surprised? Isn't there a psychology in that, having everything you want on the outside but being completely lonely on the inside?"

I shrugged.

"He seemed like a decent guy. Do you know who would want to do any harm to him?"

Susan ran her fingers through her hair.

"That was the first question the cops asked me when I got here. No, I can't think of anything."

I thought over the list of names I had drawn up from the records the night before and the one that had stood out to me the most.

"Do you know a Katie?"

Susan shook her head.

"I...I don't think so, why?"

"He talked about her in quite a few sessions, divulged he had placed a restraining order on her once, said they were..."

Susan lit up and raised her finger in the air as if an invisible lightbulb had suddenly come on.

"Fiancé..."

She chuckled and sipped her Coke.

"Oh, I remember that disaster. Like I said, we exchanged Christmas cards. That year she was on it, usually, it was some generic 'Merry Christmas, Happy New Year' on it. That year, it was one of those photo cards, the two of them smiling like idiots..."

Susan gulped the remainder of the Coke.

"I shouldn't say it like that. Maybe he was happy, but he was pushing sixty. She had to be in her twenties. Big blue eyes, long blonde hair, perky..."

Susan stopped herself.

"Sorry...it just seemed so silly. He had spent his whole life making his life about not settling down. The few short convos we had, it was always 'popped out another one, sis.' Anyways then, with no warning, this card shows up in the mail with some chick on it not only saying 'Merry Christmas' but announcing their engagement."

I wondered with wide interest about this Katie. Suddenly, it meant a lot more knowing that James had made their engagement so public, at least those closest to him.

"They broke up about two, three years ago now. I wouldn't put much credit on that. I mentioned it to the cops, but they didn't seem very interested."

I begged to differ.

"Do you know what the restraining order was about?"

Susan shrugged.

"I have no idea. I called him on his birthday to be polite, and he said they had broken up. Difference of opinion or something like that. He never mentioned the restraining order or that it was anything but amicable."

"Do you still have a copy of the card?"

Susan stood up.

"If you want to know what she looks like, feel free to sneak a peak in his room down the hall. Already gave a few pictures to the cops. He had a drawer full of some suggestable pictures of many a girlfriend, I suppose, but there were a couple of framed ones of her still up. Maybe love finally bit him in the butt."

I got to my feet.

"If you don't mind?"

"No, help yourself. Anyways, I gotta sort through the rest of this stuff before Goodwill shows up."

James's bedroom was down a short hall that had two other seemingly empty bedrooms and a bathroom. It was a large space, two windows facing the street and dressed in gray silk drapes letting in a splash of light that did nothing to lighten the dark black comforter and deep mahogany lacquered headboard with matching nightstands. Everything was still shadowy and murky in the dim light. Boxes half-filled lined one wall, and a couple trash bags sat in front of the dresser. I stopped there and peered in the top of the bag. I wasn't sure of what to make of the lacy panties and suggestive photos half-crumpled inside. The others were overflowing with a variety of clothes. I figured by the open closet doors, the place had been purged recently. I gazed at the framed photos on top of the dresser, three five by sevens of the same smiling pretty blond girl—wide smile, big blue eyes. She was a definite looker, but there seemed to be something genuine in the closeness between her and James that didn't seem staged despite their obvious age difference. I picked up the photos and traced my fingers over the one, my mind trying to wander beyond the paper. What had transpired between love and hate? If she had meant so much in his world at the time, then why had she become such a dangerous weapon? I tried hard to think about any significant conversations we had regarding Katie but realized he talked only briefly of her. I realized in James's world, that suddenly meant a lot, not mentioning his sister or parents and referring to the other women that had come in and out of his life as the girls. Katie had been something, really something. I wondered if the police had realized the significance if they had already talked to her and found nothing. I wondered if a petite, beautiful thing like that could be driven to more. I knew in my field, a broken heart doesn't always heal. I wondered how Katie must feel—his pearl, to suddenly be tossed aside and probably shortly after back to his old ways from what Susan said. James had always mentioned the girls he "dated" as the women. Katie, he had lingered two sessions on and called her by name. I had noticed distress and a lot of emotion when he had spoken of her, but by the third session, he wouldn't even mention her, and it wasn't but shortly after that, he had decided we were done. Had I hit a sore spot? Perhaps. I also realized in that moment by Susan's admission, he had no trouble jumping back on the saddle so to speak. Four women who knew him well enough to drop by his place and maybe more but still to have four relationships less than two years after Katie—had there been some animosity, some hanging on, on her part? Was it simply a case of love gone wrong, the same old song and dance of one person being unfaithful to another? That would explain Katie flying into a rage and James retaliating in a passive-aggressive way by calling the cops on her, or perhaps he really truly felt threatened, but that was neither here nor there.

"Find what you were looking for?"

I came out of the bedroom with her picture in hand. Susan was coming back in from loading a few more boxes. She brushed her hands on her jeans.

"I feel like some of this stuff is too personal to just donate, although I have no idea what I am going to do with it."

She made a show with her hands around the near-empty house save for the furniture.

"Is there anything else you can tell me about this Katie?"

Susan looked at me as if perhaps I was speaking another language.

"Everything I know of her is in that picture. James never shared much about his personal life. Getting that Christmas card was a little shocking…"

"Yet you never pried, I mean you never…"

Susan sighed, a little frustrated.

"Listen, I know about as much as you do. I would like to say I wanted to think Katie was it, but honestly, except for the ring on her finger, I just thought this too shall pass. I made that one phone call to congratulate them. He said he was going to make time for me and the kids. I never saw him or her. The next thing I know, it was over. That was my brother for you."

I flapped the picture.

"I'm sorry. You have been more than generous. I shouldn't have…"

Susan cut me off and offered a tired smile.

"I get it, okay? I hope you find whatever you're after."

"Call me for any reason."

I handed her a business card, and we parted ways. I knew enough about James to put the pieces together, but I realized I knew nothing about Katie, and that was as good a place as any to start.

# Chapter 14

Katie peered out the front window of the car and watched Michael enter James's house, and she wasn't sure whom she despised more—James's sister Susan or his therapist in that moment. She sat watching the minutes tick by, only imagining what they were discussing or what was transpiring. She had staked out the house over the course of the week. The other girls that had come and gone were excuses for women and minor mistakes James had betrayed her with shortly after they had broken up. They were not worth her time. Whatever they came looking for, they just as soon left. Michael, however, just kept messing where she didn't belong. How one woman who had no personal vested interest in James could be so tangled in his life was beyond her, and a part of her wondered if there was a bit more to the story than was being told. She waited until Michael walked out and got back in her car and headed out before she pulled back out onto the road and headed for her original destination. As she drove, her mind wandered down memory lane to a more pleasant moment in her life, the day she had met James.

James Taylor Jefferson was supposed to be it, the only man for the rest of her life. Even though he was more than twenty years her senior, he didn't look a day past thirty. He was well-built and strikingly handsome, and well, he had his shit together unlike the boys Katie was used to dating. Their meeting was that of chance, and their romance was something she had waited a very long time for, and then he had just left her, left her in the wake of everything like a ship wrecked on a distance shore. Arizona to Seattle was a day's drive, and he had been vacationing in the sunny state to get away from the bitter winter cold in the northwest. Katie worked at the Scottsdale mall in one of many luxury stores full-time on her winter break from the college nearby. She had a taste for expensive things and a goal for law school in her future. The petite platinum blonde with blue eyes could turn a lot of heads from a mile away, and James had been no different that morning when he strolled into the department store. James intrigued her. Just two days before Christmas, most people were hurriedly last-minute shopping and had a hundred places to be. He cruised the store without intention and ended up buying a silk tie.

"Special dinner tonight?"

Katie smoothed the deep green dress over her body and walked forward to the tie rack where the man stood. He was taller than her by a measurable difference, and his deep brown hair had begun to turn a salt-and-pepper gray, but his face was handsome and his hazel eyes were warm and kind. His smile widened as he caught her attention.

"If you're here to try to sell me on something, I have my mind made up already."

Katie laughed, causing him to chuckle. "What makes you think a thing like that?"

"You're clever, I'll give you that, and pretty too…"

Katie touched the rack of ties.

"So what color is the suit?"

Their eyes met.

"Black."

Katie slipped her fingers across a deep red tie.

"It is almost Christmas, ya know."

James looked at her selection.

"Sold."

Katie led him to the register, ringing up the nearly three-hundred-dollar silk necktie. It wasn't the statement of his money that drew her to him—it was his charismatic way, his character—and maybe that's what drew him to her, because he was used to women falling all over him when he flashed cash, but Katie didn't bat a pretty eyelash. She continued the transaction without hesitation.

"What time do you get off?"

Katie smiled, put off but pleasantly warmed by his offer. "Mister…"

He took the small bag from her hands.

"James."

Katie smiled again. "I suppose you're a man who is used to getting his way, but—"

He cut her off. "I simply asked a question. There was no implication."

James's smile met hers, and their gentle flirtation continued.

"Oh, of course you weren't."

He laughed, and she loved the roughness of it.

"I get off at six…"

"Perhaps I'll see you around six."

Katie shook her head and watched him head out the door, and of course, in just three short hours, as she gathered her coat and headed out the glass front doors, he stood outside, black suit and the red tie.

"So care to join me for dinner?"

Katie smiled. Her eyes peered at him and then shifted around the outdoor shopping square still bustling with shoppers. She supposed she was safe enough as long as they stuck somewhere nearby.

"Hmmm…sure…I know a great little French place nearby unless you had something in mind?"

James smiled warmly as she was the first girl who had not swooned over him. She was smart, careful, and beautiful in so many ways. She was sure of herself and seemed to know what she wanted, and he liked the strength and independence he found in her.

"You lead, and I'll follow."

The evening flickered in and out of her memory as Katie stood looking down at the gray headstone. She touched the top of it, took in a deep breath, and spoke to the crisp, cold air around her.

"You had to go and ruin it, didn't you?"

Katie pulled the black wool coat around her and headed out her black boots crunching through the stiff grass. Her eyes took in the velvet grass covered in a layer of white frost. A few people were scattered around, and a few cars drove slowly in and out, but nothing stuck out on her radar. She now tucked in her dark coat, and with the hat pulled over the brunette-colored wig, she would be hard to spot anyways. The cold made her think of the warmth she had left in Arizona, the warmth she had left from James's arms. They had had a whirlwind four months together before he placed that ring on her finger and promised her forever. She had six months remaining of college, and she had already applied for law school in Washington State. She was packing boxes in her apartment and spent long weekends and holidays at James's house. She had never felt like she was coming home until she came home to him. Katie loved James in a way that was real and she treasured…until it wasn't. Until he had gone and ruined everything over one little mistake, ripping away everything she knew, taking away the only real love she had ever felt and breaking her heart into pieces. Katie had begged and pleaded for his forgiveness. She had tried so hard to be back in his good graces, but nothing was to change, and no soon after he had left her was he back to his old ways, his old tricks, and that left a fiery fury in her like no other. There was no way come hell or high water that she was letting him walk completely off her life as if nothing had ever happened between them.

Just when she thought that she had everything all wrapped up and could hop on the nearest jet plane and leave all this behind her, that women had to come waltzing in seemingly out of the blue. The moment Michael had stuck her nose in James's business, Katie had been all over her. Such a meek woman. She had figured a good scare would set her right and to grab all and any info that James had left behind, so there were no paper trails. Unfortunately, not only had James met his end but so had her right-hand man, and now, she was left to clean up multiple messes and put out a fire before it turned into a blaze.

# Chapter 15

"Why are you even bothering sticking your nose in this at all, Michael? I'm sure if this Katie person is of any interest, the cops have already done their job."

Richard looked at her across the small metal dinner table in the corner deli, just a few blocks down from her office. Their friendship was blooming again, flourishing somehow in the ashes of their doomed romance.

"Maybe I'm afraid for my own safety…"

I looked down at the pastrami on rye, but it no longer was appealing.

"Ha, I don't think so. I know you too well. You're more curious than anything."

I leaned forward and lowered my voice to a whisper.

"That file turned up on a dead man's body after it was stolen from my office."

Richard took a bite of his sandwich looked thoughtful for a moment, before washing it down with a swig of diet Coke.

"So why Katie?"

I let out a breath I didn't realize I had been holding.

"I went over that file so many times I nearly memorized it, and she was the only person that stood out, and then after going by his house meeting with his sister, knowing who James was, all of that, Richard—she was the only one who…"

Richard cut me off.

"The only one who got close to him."

"Yes, exactly. You were friends with him for a while. Did you ever meet Katie?"

"I wouldn't call us friends, more colleagues, work associates. I have only been acquainted with him the last couple of years. You said they were…"

"Broken up for a while, maybe a year…."

Richard pushed his plate aside and mashed the straw into the ice.

"You realize the ludicrously of that, Michael. A year or more is a long time to hold a grudge."

"What if they were in contact? What if they even slept together or were romantic on some level? What if she was luring him back into her life the whole time and things didn't go as she planned, there are a whole lot of ifs there, Richard…"

"One other big if you're forgetting…"

"What exactly is that?"

"You're his therapist—or were, sorry. If he mentioned Katie in the past, then why didn't he mention her in the present? Think about it—she bothered him enough, got to him enough for him to bring it up in therapy so if there was any kind of rekindling going on, wouldn't he be looking for your opinion?"

I looked at him for a second as if he was stupid.

"What?"

He smiled and pushed his plate aside.

"Oh, come on, Richard. We didn't exactly announce it to the world. Every time we spent an evening or two together letting off steam."

Richard chuckled, but I could see the flicker in his eyes and knew it stung a little.

"Is that what you call it?"

I made a show of checking the time on my watch.

"I really have to get back to the office."

"Duty calls…"

We stood up, and the chairs made a scraping noise on the tile floor; he walked me to the door.

"Listen, thanks for listening and thanks for lunch…"

An awkward moment that we would have normally been filled with a polite hug stood between us, we hadn't made it back to that point. I almost felt like shaking his hand or stepping in and wrapping my arms around him, but I knew it just wasn't time.

"Yeah, anytime."

I watched him walk to his car and waved as he pulled out before I hurried down the block to my office. The rain had started with a light mist, and I shivered inside my wool jacket. I thought of Katie, of James, and wondered if she had been burned in the same way left in the wake of love's disaster.

I had counseled enough people and now stood on the other side of deeply hurting someone. Had Katie been left standing there, still very much in love, still hoping for a happy ending when James had cut her off? And even more so was the burning question how two people who go from engaged to split, and not only split but not amicably. I wondered about the restraining order he had placed on Katie, not something I could access. He had casually said things had gotten volatile on her part and he had feared for his safety, and if that was true, if Katie was capable of scaring a grown man, what more was she capable of?

"So the three-day rule still applies?"

I buzzed his line on the way home as I worked my way through traffic. The rush of his rough voice made my heart flutter like I was sixteen all over again, and by the soft chuckle I got in response, I felt I had the same effect on him.

"Aren't you supposed to wait for my call?"

He shot back in perfect timing.

"Okay, well played…"

We talked casually about the boring ins and outs of property sales, and his family as well as mine as I made the thirty-minute commute home. I pulled into the drive and idled the car, unclipping my seatbelt and relaxing back in the seat.

"So can I see you again before you go?" I heard myself saying.

"A second date already?"

I chuckled.

"Don't press your luck, buddy. I don't recall us having a first date."

"Ah, I forgot the friend zone…"

I laughed, but in all honesty, I didn't know what I or he was thinking. We didn't even live in the same damn state. I wasn't going anywhere near that one yet since he had crash-landed back in my life, but I couldn't stop thinking about him. How one person could change your life completely, how it could lead you to murder the very object of your affection was beyond me, but I knew in my line of work that some people completely snapped.

"How about tomorrow noon? I could use another drive out to the country."

"Sounds good. I'll see you then."

I was happy to see Maria was home earlier than expected and the aromas of spices and grilling meat greeted me.

"Hey, roomie."

I shut the door and dropped my things across the back of the sofa. Kicking my shoes off, I headed for a bottle of chilled wine.

"Junior Detective. What's up?"

I fished out a glass and poured it half full of red, took a sip, and leaned against the counter. Maria was out of uniform, dressed in a pair of denim jeans that brought out her curves nicely and a black sweater that accented well her accents. I laughed internally at my cleverness.

"I should ask you, hot date, should I hide in my room?"

Maria finished flipping the meat and turned toward me.

"What can't cook dinner for a friend?"

I laughed.

"I'm not biting. I'm gonna go change."

I finished a second gulp of wine and felt my head buzz and my stomach growl. I realized it had been a long time since lunch, and I had hardly finished that anyways. I was kinda glad my best friend was in the kitchen cooking supper at that moment and maybe I could pry out some answers to my own questions. I hurried upstairs and quickly exchanged my day clothes for a pair of flannel pants and an oversized T-shirt that sported UW from my college days.

"Sorry, I'm not dressing up for you."

I chuckled and sat down at the small table as Maria brought over platters of grilled chicken and fragrant-smelling white rice—my guess, jasmine—and bread, as if that was not enough carbs.

"Well, I came home and changed before I headed to the store. We seem to live like a couple of bachelorettes."

I got up and brought over my wine the bottle and a second glass.

"Speaking of bachelorettes, things get hot and heavy with you and the old fling?"

I took a bite of chicken and pointed my fork at her.

"You wish. He heads back to California Sunday. Even if I wanted to go there, I'm not one for long-distance relationships. I have enough complications in my life. If I ever decided to date again, it's gotta be simple and straightforward."

"Well, that's quite a statement to make over a 'friend.'"

We shared a short laugh, and I finished off my glass of wine.

"Anyways, back to what I was saying. Turns out this Katie person was a big deal in James's life. I went by his old house, ran into his sister…"

Maria looked at me in surprise.

"More snooping, seriously? If you're concerned about your own safety, you should go to the police."

I munched on a bite of rice and looked at her.

"I have…point aside, I got a lot of valuable information. I think Katie was a bigger component in his life than I knew. I only wish I could get my hands on that restraining order he filed or any other information."

"The order wasn't filed here?"

"No, in Arizona. I guess they lived there briefly. She had an apartment. The deal was for her to finish school. She had like six months left to graduate—that's what I seem to gather—then they were moving back to his house here in Washington, but it never got around to that. Somewhere in there, he must have filed the order, and they parted ways after that. What I don't get is that he said, and I wrote in my notes that Katie was his one biggest mistake. He spilled the beans about here in two sessions, and that was it. That's why at first I didn't give any weight to the matter, and now looking back, I realize she was the only one he talked about. I didn't even know he had a sister until I ran into her, not even on any intake forms he filled out did he mention her."

"Which means he was a pretty private person, didn't like to share. Do you remember how he seemed when he talked about her?"

"He always talked about her in the past, if that's what you mean."

She poured some wine and mixed her chicken and rice thoughtfully with her fork.

"So he came to therapy for how long?"

"A year."

"Then eight months ago, roughly at the end of that year, he quit therapy?"

"That's correct. Are we getting to a point here, Officer?"

"When was the last time he spoke to her?"

"Well, it would have been—oh, two years—so he would have broken up with her three months after he started therapy with me."

"Bingo."

"You think his initial regard for therapy was Katie. He never let on to that, just said he was there to talk. I can look at my notes, but I think it was several months into the sessions that he even brought her up when I asked about relationships. He just mentioned his casual affairs with women, how he wasn't one to settle down, whether his depression and anxiety was caused by a horrible breakup really is beside the point. That's neither here nor there."

"True, but you ever wonder if they came back together for a makeup session or at least one party tried to fuel the fire."

I pondered that for the moment.

"No, I think it was exactly the opposite. Susan said at least four women came by the house after James passing, inquiring on his money and his property. Who knows if there was more? So maybe he was cheating on her shortly after the engagement. Maybe she found out and flew into a rage."

Maria swallowed a bite of food.

"Which would explain the restraining order, but it sounds like James had a lot of women who could have had it out for him."

I sighed.

"True, but Katie is the only one who seems to be hanging on from my perspective, the file being planted. All of that was personal Maria. Sure, people kill for money, but they weren't married to him. The only way they would have gained anything was through robbery. Anyways, Katie could very easily have a personal vendetta. I put my cards on that motive more at this point."

"True, and you are the expert in the matters of the brain."

She cracked a smile at me, and I scoffed at her. "Oh, quit. What is that supposed to mean?"

Maria shrugged. "Nothing."

"I know I haven't always been the expert in the area of love, but I'm definitely an expert in a matter of what happens when things go wrong—and it sounds like something went very wrong."

I got up and gathered our plates and headed to the kitchen sink. Maria quickly shifted gears.

"So speaking of love life, how are things between you and Richard anyways?"

"We are comfortably headed back to the friend zone, and I made it perfectly clear that's where we are staying…"

Maria chuckled and grabbed her wine glass and mine. I met her in the living room, grabbed a blanket, and sank into a corner of the sofa opposite where she was in the chair.

"Until one of you gives into temptation. Oh right, you have new temptation…"

I tossed a throw pillow at my friend.

"Well, speaking for the side of the law, if there is enough evidence, the detectives will do their job."

I finished my wine.

"Well, I'm not sitting around waiting to see what card gets dealt next. First, I nearly get framed for one man's murder and tied to another's. I swear sometimes I think the damn cops are watching me, no offense."

"None taken."

"I'm just waiting. I feel like I'm waiting for the next big thing to happen."

## Chapter 16

He never failed to amaze me even after all these years. He was standing there in a pair of faded blue jeans, scuffed cowboy boots, and a black thermal that accented his muscular chest, but it was his slow, curved smile that made my heart flutter. It didn't matter how many years had come and gone between us; he could still leave me completely undone at the sight of him. After all these years, after Richard and a handful of other lovers, no one made me feel as complete as I did in the moment I was standing in this man's presence. A part of me wanted to climb back in my car and speed off a hundred miles away from him, and the other part of me wanted to run into his arms, which is exactly the part that scared me the most. I wondered how Katie must have felt and wondered if despite their age difference, she had had the same reaction to James, as if his presence alone had left her heart in a mess of emotion and feeling. I knew as a therapist from the clinic side of things that love was a powerful magnet and a dangerous weapon in the wrong hands.

"Hey, cowboy..."

I climbed out of the car and slammed the door. The gravel parking lot overlooked the rush of the sparkling blue water. Nearly bare willow trees lined the opposing shore and created a perfect backdrop against cool sunny blue skies. A chill climbed off the water, wrapping around me and penetrating through the layers of my burgundy sweater and long-sleeved tee. I couldn't help but feel a bit awkward meeting him here by the river's edge, a place we had played as children.

"So what do you have in mind?"

The sun was still bright in the blue sky, and I tucked my hands in my pocket.

"Coffee?"

"Sure…"

We headed across the street to the bed and breakfast and bought two steaming cups of large coffees in Styrofoam cups and walked back across to the River. The soft sand made my boots sink in, and I wobbled a bit as I headed for the more stable rocky bed, better for such winter footwear. Chris chuckled, and I felt his hand on my waist steadying me before the coffee, and I took a sudden spill.

"Thanks."

I was aware of his gaze as it locked with mine. Before I moved away from his touch, walking along the shoreline, sipping the hot liquid, I finally found a smooth place the sun directly touched and sat down. Chris sat beside me close enough that I could feel the warmth of his body but far enough away to be respectful. Even if I wasn't single, it would take all of heaven and earth not for me to throw the coffee aside and sink into his arms, but I also knew what dangerous territory that was. I wondered idly why I had come here, knowing where it could possibly lead.

"I never thought we would be like this again…"

I looked up at him, and he smiled.

"I know. I'm glad I ran into you."

His gaze didn't leave mine, and this time, he didn't ask. His fingers swept a lock of hair from my face, sending a shiver down my spine, and before I could utter a word of protest, his lips were on mine. I hesitated against him for a second, and then I felt my whole body sigh. My eyes slipped closed and my mouth slipped open, and I tasted him again. Even after all these years, some things never changed. I felt his hand on my waist again, and I lifted up a tad until my chest sank against his, and for a moment, time stood still. For a moment, I felt like I had come home. After a long, breathless second, we parted ways, and both of us laughed awkwardly.

"I'm sorry, I don't…"

I picked my coffee cup back up and sipped it then wrapped both my hands around it, before I felt myself doing anything foolish.

"It's okay. I…"

I felt him come towards me again and pressed my free hand against his chest before a silly childhood fantasy got us in real trouble.

"Chris, cowboy, I…I can't, I'm sorry."

"Mmmm, baby, I never knew how much I missed you until I found you."

His lips brushed my cheek, and for a second, I almost gave in. This time, I stood up on my feet and gained some space between us.

"I'm sorry, Michael. I…"

He stood up to join me.

"I'm not angry. I just…you have your life and I have mine, and well, you're…"

"Leaving again."

I sighed. I didn't want to say it, but I was glad he did, and I realized no matter how older and wiser we were, some things never changed.

"Chris, I…"

He touched my hand, his fingers lingering with mine for a brief second.

"It's different this time. What if we…"

I smiled.

"Chris, I think we should just…I want to stay in touch, I do, but I think we should just be friends."

"After that…"

We both laughed at the joke, and it felt good to break the tension.

"Were not kids anymore. Sometimes it's easy to get caught up in a moment. There is a part of us that always wants to go back, but it's just not possible."

I stared out at the river bubbling along, and for some reason, I couldn't look right at him. He got up and skipped a stone into the water.

"Michael, I don't want your therapy bullshit. At least be honest with me…"

I looked at him, realizing in that moment he was the one who had left, who had abandoned me with a broken heart. Long forgotten anger collided with a passion that was damn hard to deny. I turned and looked at him.

"I don't know, Chris. I never imagined us like this again, but here we are, and yes, I have feelings for you. Is it momentary passion, or is it something real? I don't know, but I have my life and you have yours, and well, I don't want a bunch of complications. I have enough on my plate as is."

Chris looked at me for a long second before responding, I imagined Katie on the threshold waiting for an answer from James, every dream and desire she had in her aching heart broken into a million pieces in a split second.

"I can't say the same thing, Michael, but I do know I made my own choices as well, not trying to find you all these years and leaving you hanging all those years ago…"

I sighed and touched his arm.

"Please, we were kids. I don't hold any hard feelings over that…"

Our eyes touched, and all I wanted was to slide right back in his arms again.

"Friends?"

I put my hand out casually, and he shook it briefly. We both laughed.

"Okay, friends…"

We collected our cups and headed back up the river bank to our cars, I watched him pull away in his truck before I headed out. I wondered if I would ever actually see him again or if we would naturally drift apart this time. Suddenly, my heart and mind were at war with one another. My thoughts were suddenly interrupted as the music on my radio cut out and a call buzzed in.

"Hello?" I answered hesitantly.

"I have been watching you. Don't think I haven't been, and you better stay back if you know what's good for you."

My heart stopped cold. My car moved a tad out of its lane as I hit the curves of the back road on my way out to the highway. One name leapt into my brain like sudden fire.

"Katie?"

There was a pause before the female voice spoke again.

"This is your only warning. Next time, don't consider yourself so lucky."

The line went instantly dead. I pulled off the road for a brief second. Pure instinct made me check the screen on the phone, though logic told me otherwise. Let's just say I wasn't surprised to find the number blocked. I wonder if she had my number. Literally, what else did she have, and better yet, where was she?

Across town at a local quick stop and gas station, Katie let out long breath and broke the prepaid phone in half and tossed it in a nearby trash can. The station was adjacent to the bed and breakfast where she had watched the pair gather their coffee and head back to the riverbank. She wondered if Michael had a clue that she had been following her like a hawk. In fact, it hadn't been too hard to find out where she lay her head every night and where she worked, where she liked to lunch and her favorite coffee shop. What had started as trying to keep one suspicious woman off her trail had become a near obsession. The more she learned of Michael, the less she liked her. Why James had sought out therapy from her was beyond her reasonable thought, and what made her seethe even more was the fact that James had spread all those viscous rumors about her, painting a picture of herself that was far from the truth. Katie mused over the fact she should be back in Arizona at this point, putting in her resignation at work, tying up a few loose ends, and getting the heck out of dodge. Damn this woman for putting a big kink in her plans. Time to set her straight, so to speak.

## Chapter 17

"I was able to get a copy of the arrest record. It wasn't easy though."

Maria slapped the file down on the coffee table in front of me.

"So I owe you for life?"

Maria chuckled.

"Let's hope you don't owe me a job. I really don't know why you wanted me to go to such lengths for this. The police are there for a reason, Micky. If Katie is a suspect at all, she is already on their radar. They have all the information, and besides, I don't see how having this is going to help in any way, shape, or form."

I spun the file around, tapped my fingernails for a moment, and then looked up at Maria.

"She called today?"

Maria's eyes shot around the apartment. I felt her defenses go up quickly.

"Katie?"

"Yes. I mean she didn't identify herself, but I'm pretty damn certain it was her, and right after I met with Chris, it was like she was following me…"

"Micky, it's best you get your nose out of her business and go back to the detectives and let them handle this one."

I shook my head.

"That's what she is expecting. It will drive her farther away. This is a score to settle, a vendetta I got to close, and now she…"

Maria cut me off.

"Has it in for you—that's exactly my point."

I smirked at her.

"Nice to have a cop as a roommate."

"Don't pull that card on me, roomie."

Maria got up and headed upstairs to shower and change, I surmised. I picked up the file folder and delved into Katie's stats. First, a background check revealed nothing surprising, and her DMV record only held a few minor traffic violations. Her residence was listed as an apartment near where she attended school. It looked like she graduated last year. A potential law student, she hadn't applied to any law schools. She had no next of living kin. Looks like I had hit a solid wall. The second set of paperwork in the file was the order of protection filed against Katie Pearson by James Jefferson, and that had a lengthy trail of court records and lawyers. Looks like James even got fancy serving a protection order. The original police record was a call James made to the police department in Tempe Arizona around six in the evening on March 2—a Saturday, I casually noted. Not too surprising was the fact it was a domestic disturbance call. A little surprising but not unheard of was Katie was acting physically volatile to James, throwing things and screaming. She was hauled off that night for a brief stint in jail, and they parted ways. I assumed the order of protection followed, and of course, they parted ways.

"How's it going?"

So lost in thought, Maria made me nearly jump out of my skin as she reappeared in the living room, looking more comfortable in stretch pants and an oversized tee. Her curls were damp and loose, framing her face.

"Not much, no prior criminal record, a few speeding tickets, no next of kin listed. Looks like she graduated top of her class from Arizona state, works for a store over at the Scottsdale mall, still employed there as the general manager. Looks like she took a couple stabs at applying for law school but no follow through."

Maria sank down to the sofa.

"Yeah, she's pretty squeaky clean for someone that is a suspected murderer…"

I looked up at Maria.

"Love can make you do crazy things. I have seen how the brain can tick. You put a gun in the right hands, I'm sure a lot can go wrong, and as a cop, I'm sure you have witnessed that firsthand. One juicy tidbit of information—it wasn't the cops who served the restraining order. Looks like James paid out of pocket for a private processer to serve it for him and not just any processer—his lawyer he kept on retainer."

"Interesting…"

"Speaks volumes about how he thought of her, not only spending his own money but using someone he valued and trusted to some degree. He had some deep personal feelings toward Katie and not anything pleasant in that moment."

I sighed and checked the clock.

"Retail is open late, definitely close to the holiday season…"

I snatched up my cell phone, and Maria grabbed the remote.

"I'm gonna try to do a little relaxing before I'm back on shift again."

I googled the number for Barneys and headed upstairs to my bedroom. A chirpy voice answered on the third ring, and I asked for Katie by name.

"I'm sorry, but Miss Pearson is on a vacation at the moment. She should be back next week. Would you like to leave a message, or perhaps I can help you with something?"

Interesting fact of the night, but nowhere near surprising.

"Is there perhaps another manager I can speak with?"

"Yes, just a moment please."

A momentary pause, and then a smooth, young male voice filled the silence.

"May I help you, Miss, um…?"

"Michael is fine. I was calling in regards to Miss Pearson."

"Yes, she is on vacation till next week, but I would be happy to help."

The world of retail—and expensive retail at that. I had done my own stint behind the register in my college days, and I knew well how it worked and how trying it could be. How did I tread lightly without opening too many doors at once?

"Well, I'm calling on behalf of the police, and…"

I had already put my foot in dark waters. Thankfully, the man at the other end of the line was ahead of me.

"Oh yes, I heard about that poor man. Police already called looking for Katie. I guess he was her ex or something anyways. Like I told them, she's on vacation. I'm not sure what else I can do for you either. Poor Katie, I wonder if she even knows. To know somebody and then…just tragic."

"Yes, it sure is."

I pushed forward.

"How long has Katie been employed there?"

"I'm not really sure. I came on a year ago, but she helped train me, so I figure a few years before that…"

Long sigh.

"Listen, I'd love to help, but like I told the detectives, it's best to ask Katie these. Oh god, she's not like a suspect or something?"

The voice rose in pitch.

"No, we're just, um, gathering as much information as possible from those who knew her best."

"Well, I'll be happy to let her know you called. May I have your name?"

I faked static on the line and quickly hung up. I lay back across the bed and let out a long breath. That did not go as smoothly as I had hoped or planned and left me no closer to finding out exactly who Katie was than I was before. I wondered suddenly where she was and what she was doing. Perhaps after a few threats, she felt her job was done and she was on a plane to Mexico or some other far-off destination. I got up and padded over to the dresser. I snatched up the photo I had taken of the happy couple and sat back down on the end of the bed. I looked intensely for a long moment at the short, petite blonde with long locks and deep blue eyes. She didn't seem threatening in any way, but I knew in my line of work, looks were always deceiving. I contemplated their life together as a couple and the love that seemed to be displayed in picture-perfect smiles in a five-by-seven photo. Could Katie really be the one who had brought James life to a tragic end? Most likely, by physical stature alone, I guessed she had help. The idea of help led me back to the man that had been found in the alley with my file folder, whoever he had been in life, what connection did he have to Katie. I mulled over the many-faceted angles, the puzzle pieces before me, and then picked up my phone and did the good old Google and FB search. Lo and behold, blond, blue-eyed Katies were not in short supply, but nothing really pinged the radar. I suppose in the world of *Big Brother*, as easily as someone could be found, they just as easily could hide behind a facade. I clicked off and headed back downstairs. My head had begun to ache, and I knew I had done enough digging for the moment.

"So any new clues?"

Maria got up and placed her bowl in the sink.

"Not really, but I think I know what I need to do next."

"Oh yeah, and what's that?"

"Take a little trip to Arizona."

The spoon clattered into the bowl, and Maria came over to where I sat. She looked at me for a long second as if she wasn't sure what she should say or do. Thankfully, she knew me well enough.

"You know I'm not gonna tell you what to do, but you know how I feel."

I sighed.

"I know and I appreciate the concern, but I just feel there is more to the story that needs to be told. Something doesn't sit right with me."

I drummed my fingers thoughtfully on the counter.

"Besides, what am I supposed to do—sit around here and wait for her next move?"

"Her next move? What are you thinking, Sherlock?"

"The man in the alley was most likely her right-hand man—that goes without saying."

Maria nodded.

"True, but he's also dead."

I chuckled.

"I'm beginning to think Katie has a way with men."

Maria laughed.

"She seems pretty fierce."

"She seems responsible for murder," I quickly pointed out.

Maria shot back just as fast, "Which is exactly why you shouldn't go chasing after her. Let the police do their job."

## Chapter 18

Before heading for Arizona, there was one last thing I needed to do. In case I could gather any more tidbits of information, I had arranged to meet with James's lawyer, who had ultimately served Katie with the order of protection. The coffee shop sat in a busy neighborhood district and served not only those on their way to and from work but many bicyclists, walkers, and mothers with tots in strollers, and there was plenty of those to be had this morning as the relentless wet cold rolled back warm blue skies with wisps of soft white clouds. I pulled into a parking spot next to a gleaming white Mercedes, just like Ron had said for me to look for. I got out and headed into the shop.

"Thanks for meeting me on short notice."

Dishes clattered, machines hissed, toddlers cried, and voices mixed in highs and lows, everything you would expect from a morning rush. Ron sat amidst it all, tapping away on his phone and sipping some high-priced concoction. He looked up as I sat down.

"Sure, although I still don't entirely know what this is about or how I can help you. You're James's therapist, correct? Do you work with the police?"

That was it—no friendly introduction all, business. I sat down and proceeded.

"Not exactly. I just had a few questions, I thought you might be able to answer for me in interest of his ex-fiancée Katie…and the order of protection you served her."

I paused and let the silence linger over the name. I looked for any reaction in his expression but failed to see any. Instead, he smiled.

"Ah, so that's what this is about. Yes, I serve as a private processor on occasion for my clients. Mostly, I'm a real estate attorney first. I provided legal guidance for James in the purchase and sale of his properties."

The chair scooted back, and I realized I had pushed too many buttons perhaps.

"Listen, I'm due in court soon. The police have already interviewed me. I'm not sure how else I can help. He was a client, one I had for many years, but I didn't really have any personal involvement."

I held up my hand.

"Please, just a few more questions."

The chair stopped pushing back.

"James called and asked me for a favor. He paid double my fees and my travel expenses to go to Arizona to serve Katie with the order."

"Doesn't that seem a little far-fetched to you? I mean, couldn't he have had the police do it?"

Ron shrugged.

"Sure, I suppose, but listen, I deal with a lot of high-priced clientele. They don't play small. James started out on the bottom, but he was good. He worked his way up quickly, he was making six figures pretty fast, and he was like most of the guys. I knew he dealt with things on his own terms. I honestly didn't care. I wasn't doing anything illegal. I was paid a hefty sum to serve paperwork—getting it done was all that mattered to me."

"So you knew nothing about Katie or their relationship?"

Ron shook his head. "No, he just called me one day and asked for me to serve her the papers, gave me the info, sent a check—that was about it." Ron made a show of checking his watch. "Really, I should be going."

"Yes, of course. One last thing?"

"Sure."

"How did Katie seem when you served her?"

Ron smiled. "How do you think? Her ex-fiancé was serving her with an order of protection. It's usually the female against the male.

She was visibly upset." Ron stood up this time and collected his coffee cup, letting me know our conversation was over.

"You're sure there is nothing else you can tell me?"

He stopped mid-stride and met my gaze. "Listen, I wish I could help you—I really do—but James was a private person. He was always about business when we met, and that's fine. With me, some guys or gals, they want to talk about their kids, their dogs, send you a Christmas card, make a connection. James didn't, and I was fine with that the bills get paid—that's all that matters."

I let him go at that and sighed, joining the crowd and grabbing the largest cup of sugary iced coffee I could stand. I had exactly twenty-two hours ahead of me, traversing parts of Oregon, Idaho, and Utah, and I was very much regretting taking a buddy with me for company, although I wasn't sure anyone would join me in my madness. Even my own brain was trying to give me an eviction notice.

* * *

The hours slipped by with several packs of gum, a bit of traffic, and long stretches of unbroken road with nothing to see for miles except truckers hauling their loads. The weather went between showers that forced me to click my wipers to high and sunshine so bright I had to pull over to search the car for my sunglasses. Bathroom stops, food stops, and gas stops rounded things out. Night had settled into shades of gray over the flat desert land of burnt sienna dirt and wildflowers. The weather had climbed into the seventies, and I had gone down from a sweater and jacket to a T-shirt. My butt was numb, my legs ached, and I couldn't feel my toes. I hadn't done anything crazy like this since my college years, and I was feeling it as I finally hit the border of Arizona, leaving the rest up to tomorrow. I pulled into the nearest motel, a two-story brown stucco abode with a sign lit up in green reading "Holiday Inn." I smiled at the thought of showering and stretching out on a large bed, as I parked and headed for the reservation desk. Thankfully, it was the off season and not making a reservation in advance didn't do anything from keeping me from a room. I reparked the car closer to my room and slipped my duffel bag over my shoulder and grabbed my laptop. Using the back door, I headed down the thick carpeted hallway until I reached my room. Ever so grateful, I swung open the door and stepped inside. The usual setup greeted me, and I sank face down across the cool mattress with an audible sigh.

## Chapter 19

After showering, changing into some comfy clothes, and grabbing coffee and a muffin from the breakfast bar, I headed out into the warm sunshine a break from the blustery cold of fall in the NW. My first stop was Scottsdale, the Beverly Hills of Arizona. The main mall was white and cream stone work that housed the most high-end jewelry and designer clothes available, classy restaurants, lush green parks, and giant stucco houses in shades of tan with palm trees lining the drives, and well-manicured front lawns along the nearby streets rounded things out.

Barneys, where Katie had clocked the hours between school and home, was one of the stores that had an outside entrance and, no surprise, offered valet service. I had dressed down in a pair of jeans and black T-shirt and tennis shoes and suddenly felt underdressed for the entire place. Parking in a nearby lot, I strolled up to the front entrance with as much confidence as I could muster, pretty sure I couldn't afford a sock in this place.

"May I help you?"

I was commandeered by a pretty young woman in slacks and a silk blouse smelling strongly of a fragrant floral perfume. I met her warm brown eyes that seemed to give me the once over, her blonde tresses pinned back from a pretty face.

"Yes, actually, I was wondering if Katie was working?"

I saw the disappointment behind the smile and wondered if the employees worked solely on commission.

"Paul is our manager on the floor today. Would you like to speak with him?"

I nodded and followed her swaying hips and clacking heels across tiled floors. Racks of good slacks, silk dresses, blouses, etc., were well-placed on shelves around the store where women shopped with vested interest.

"Paul, this young lady would like to speak with you."

Paul was a colored gentleman of tall stature, well-polished in a charcoal-gray suit and black tie. He turned hesitantly in my direction. I think he knew as well as the woman that I wasn't there to shop.

"Yes, may I help you?"

I clasped my hands in front of my waist.

"I'm here to inquire about Katie Pearson…"

Paul made a scoffing noise and stopped folding shirts.

"Oh please, that girl. Yes, best sales rep here, took a vacation and then never returned to work."

So there had been an update in the few days since I had made my original phone call.

"Not that I'm complaining. I filled those shoes, kind of a job promotion…" Paul turned to face me. "But the suddenness of it, ya know…so weird. She had worked here for a while too, but I guess you never know." Paul waved his hand in the air. "And the police, you're not with them?"

Paul's eyes grew wide.

"Um not exactly." I lied with ease that surprised myself.

"Listen, they came. I told them everything I could. I don't know what else I can tell you. I'm sorry."

Paul suddenly busied himself with a rack of silk scarfs. I feigned interest in a cranberry-and-green patterned one and ran it through my fingertips.

"Gorgeous, isn't it? One of our newest additions."

Without looking at the price tag, I snagged it. "I'll take it."

Drawing his interest back to me, he suddenly ushered me over to a rack of blouses. I settled on a pale blue one, and we headed for the register. A mere six hundred dollars later, I owned the most expensive clothes of my life and the personal information of Miss Katie Pearson.

"Thank you, Paul."

He nodded.

"Of course. Anytime."

I gathered my bag and left, eliciting a cold stare from the woman who had originally helped me. I smiled for the hell of it, swung my bag, and left the store. My stomach growled right on cue, and I decided I had enough with this place. I got back in my car and drove away toward the University, stopping nearby for a quick bite before I headed to Katie's home address.

* * *

A set of four gray boxes, each housing half a dozen apartments, palm trees fronted a gray unlocked iron gate, the illusion of security. I pulled in and circled through the various parking spaces until I found the C building and a visitors' parking slot. I double-checked the apartment number on my phone and headed to the second floor, apartment 220. A dark bluish-gray door with a gold knocker greeted me. I could hear the flow of music and voices filtering from doors down the hallway. Place like this probably housed a lot of college students. I took a breath and knocked, not hoping for much. A second knock after a moment of silence elicited a muffled male voice, and I was greeted by a man in his twenties, his hair rumpled, and his well-muscled form filled out the tank and plaid boxers. I was assured I had woken him from sleep.

"Sorry to disturb you, but—"

He flashed a lopsided smile, and I felt his eyes roam over me. "No disruption at all. What can I help you with?"

I wondered if I should play into his cheap flirtatious charm or push back and become offended. I offered him a warm smile instead.

"I'm looking for an old friend. Maybe you know her. Name's Katie…Katie Pearson. This was her last known address. Phone number is out of order. I was in the area, so I thought—"

He shrugged indifferently. "Nope, sorry. Maybe she was the old renter. Don't know—I just moved in the first of the month couple weeks ago. Maybe the landlord knows…"

"Thank you for your help."

I turned around to leave and heard his voice call after me.

"Hope you find what you're looking for."

I heard the door shut and was grateful. Heading back to the parking lot, I crossed it to the main office, but it was just my luck that a "be back soon" hung in the window. I sighed in frustration and contemplated my next move when a slim female with spiky black and blue hair approached me, a basket of laundry tucked under one arm, well-tanned brown skin in a pair of gray sweats.

"Are you looking for a Katie?"

I looked at her in surprise as if she was some telepath that had read my mind. The young woman chuckled.

"Neighbor. Overheard you talking to El Macho when I was stepping out to get my wash…"

We shared a laugh together at that point.

"Yeah, he's, uh, something else…"

The young women started walking.

"Follow me up. Not sure I can help you out much—she moved out a couple weeks ago. I have no idea where she went. We weren't BFFs or anything, had a few classes together at the U. She was looking for a place to crash when I met her. So I told her there were places available but I didn't know of anyone looking for a roommate."

I followed her across the parking lot and back up the stairs.

"Don't mind the mess, not all my roommates are as neat as me."

I stepped into the typical college pad of any young twenty-something living on a budget—black futon, secondhand store coffee table in lacquered wood, and a large flat-screen TV—but it was neat and clean with a few soft, feminine touches.

"I heard that?"

Another young female smiled under a mop of blond curls, dressed in jeans and a dark-green tank top. She grabbed a light jacket and a backpack.

"I got class, Carrie. I'm out. See you later." She stopped when she turned and saw me. "Who's this?"

I extended my hand, and she shook it hesitantly.

"This is, um…"

"Michael." I filled in the blank.

"Interesting choice for a name. Can't say I have heard that one recently…"

The one with the blond mop that wasn't Carrie had no problem stating her opinion. I hoped her Chatty Cathy ways would turn out to be a good thing and work in my favor.

"Sydney, what's up?"

Carrie plopped the laundry basket on the futon.

"She was inquiring about Katie to our new neighbor."

Sydney made a scoffing sound and rolled her eyes.

"Katie was definitely a better neighbor, just a little odd."

I stepped into the opening as Carrie began to fold clothes in the background.

"Odd how?"

She shrugged and pulled gum out of her pack and began to chew noisily.

"Well, just different—two-bedroom apartment and she moves in on her own. Girl had some money, I guess—she was always dressed well. Then again, she could have been getting a massive discount. Heard she worked for Barneys. She was polite enough but always very quiet, ya know, in and out, school and work. We invited her over for parties, never wanted to come. Never really had any guests until, well…"

Sydney looked to Carrie for confirmation on that one. Carrie stopped folding shirts.

"The guy. Yeah, he looked old enough to be her dad. We thought maybe that answered the large apartment and the money thing. He showed up a few months after she moved in. She was farther ahead in school than we were at the time she moved in, so we assumed maybe she had been living some other place. She never really talked a lot about herself or her situation."

Sydney popped a bubble.

"I gotta run before I'm late for class. Nice meeting you."

Sydney stepped out the front door, leaving the two of us solo.

"You're not an old friend, are you?"

Carrie stopped mechanically folding laundry and looked at me suddenly. I wasn't sure how to read her gaze, but the friendliness had started to leave and a new wind had blown in.

"Why do you say that?"

Carrie sighed.

"I study law, almost thought of being a cop once, ended up going a different route. Besides, you ask too many questions for someone that should know someone a little bit and…"

Carrie paused as if she had said too much.

"And?"

"The cops came by shortly after she split, asked a few questions, a lot less than you did, wouldn't say why. Care to tell me, are you some sort of private investigator?"

I let out a breath I had been holding.

"Not a private investigator, but yes, she was involved in a murder, or possibly I guess at this point."

Carries eyes got big.

"Wow, a girl like that. Nah, you got the wrong gal. She was odd, yes, but the sweetest person. Who was it?"

"James, her ex-fiancé."

Carrie got up and collected a Coke from the fridge and offered me one, but I declined.

"Ah, Mr. Money Bags…"

"Um, I guess."

Carrie took a healthy swallow and came back over to the futon and sat down. She offered me a seat, and being polite, I moved some textbooks and a laptop and sat down in an overstuffed armchair.

"That's what we called him. I let her know about the apartment she moved in, and then less than two months later, he shows up. He always came around in the evenings, never saw him on the weekends or anything, always seemed in and out. Not like we paid attention, it's just they didn't seem to spend a lot of time here. We always heard him coming and going at odd times, and the one time I did run into him, he had but two words to say to me. I guess I'm just assuming shit at this point, really. Maybe he was married. Maybe it was the age difference. Maybe they were both just busy."

Carrie stopped trailing off and took another sip of the Coke.

"Can I ask you about one night in particular?"

"Sure. See how good my memory is?"

"March second, a Saturday a couple years ago. You might remember this night. James called the cops on Miss Katie. Domestic disturbance?"

She paused. Her eyebrows arched. I knew she was racking her brain, and I wasn't sure she would come up with much, but I was pleasantly surprised.

"I do recall one night, there was a lot of yelling and sounded like things were breaking. Yeah, I was home studying for something. It was pretty quiet. Most people were out, and well, there was never much noise from her place than the door opening and shutting. The next thing I knew, cop cars. I poked my head out for a moment. Looked like things were under control, so I didn't go over there, didn't want to get in her business. I do remember it because it seemed so odd, a couple like that. I don't recall seeing much of James after that…"

I paused.

"But you saw him after that night?"

"Yeah. I figured they were making up. That's why I didn't think much of that night. I was coming home, saw him at her door, bunch of roses in his hand. Not sure what happened after. That was the last time I saw him, very rarely spoke to Katie after that, and she moved out pretty soon after."

I mused over the new information.

"I've said enough. Anyways, how do you know Katie?"

"I don't really know her per se. I was James's therapist."

Carrie chuckled.

"Well, that's different. What's his ex-therapist doing down in Arizona investigating his former fiancée?"

"Perhaps you should have been a cop," I offered with a smile.

"Maybe I'll try out again. We shall see. Anyways?"

"Long story…"

Carrie blinked as if to say "I got all the time in the world" and I realized I wasn't as easily backing out of this one.

"I don't have any morning classes today, so spill it. I always thought Katie was just a very private person, but now there seems to be more to the story. Was he married?" Carrie trailed off. Her eyes got big again.

I shook my head and laughed comically. "Believe me, I wasn't involved with James in any way. Let's just say I vested a personal interest after some rather unfortunate events entangled me in this whole business."

Carrie set the Coke down with a clink that seemed louder than it should be.

"So she is following you or threatening you or both? I still don't see how she could have anything to do with anything so violent, especially with someone she seemed to love. As odd as they were, they seemed a sweet couple…although like I said, the way he sneaked around, I wouldn't be surprised if he had a wife or another lover. I told the cops the same thing."

I began to wonder if James had a secret identity I knew nothing about, but the way Katie kept popping up, the more I snooped, the guilty finger was pointed directly at her. I stood up suddenly.

"I probably should get going. Maybe I'll head to the university next."

Carrie got up and showed me to the door.

"Good luck with that. She was pretty studious from the class we took together. Always sat in front, taking a thousand notes, and the minute the bell buzzed, she was all businesslike."

I stood on the threshold of the door.

"Not a social butterfly?"

"Only when she had to be, from what I witnessed."

"Have the name of the class or the professor by any chance?"

She paused for a moment.

"Sure. Mrs. Whitaker."

I thanked Carrie for the information and headed back across to the office to see if the manager was back in. It seemed like a good day for an extended break or a laundry list of errands. The sign still hung, and the blinds were still closed. I headed back to my car, giving Maria a quick call like I promised.

"Thank God you're still alive. Find anything out, Junior Detective?"

"I'm fine, Maria. Thanks for the concern."

I pulled out onto the main road and switched her to Bluetooth.

"I did actually find out some interesting information to say the least. The cops came by Maria's old place."

"Oh?"

I listened to noise in the background and figured she was at work, as I pulled out onto the main road and headed back toward the university. Blue skies against tan hills and lush tropical cacti. I kept my eyes peeled for a coffee shop, needing more than the watered-down hotel coffee.

"Sorry, you're at work."

"I got a second, so that's good. The cops are on her trail. Time for you to pull back, roomie."

I sighed and pulled into the drive-through and ordered a large triple mocha.

"No, time for me to up my game. I still have a vested interest in this, and I'm not pulling out, not when I feel like I'm this close…"

Maria interjected as I headed for the university, maneuvering my way around the multiple parking lots till I found a spot adjacent to the entrance. "Like I said, what are you going to do when you find her? If you do. Really, this is for your own good."

I heard Maria's voice shift to answer someone in the background.

"Listen, I gotta go. Call me later tonight, and stay safe please, okay?"

"Yes, Mom."

She chuckled at the comment, and I pushed the Off button on the Bluetooth, took a couple of sips off my coffee, and then got out and headed toward the front entrance.

# Chapter 20

Arizona State lay like a gem against a backdrop of brown hills and blue skies, just faintly dotted with wisps of white clouds. The front entrance was an old stucco building in old tech Mex style, the remaining campus spread out behind from older architectural masterpieces and low-lying one-level buildings in different shades of rustic browns and orange. I strolled up the walkway to the front entrance. Students scampered this way and that, faces lost in their smartphones, laptops and pads strung over shoulders. A few likely romantic pairs and friends intermingled. It felt like yesterday I had been on the UW campus just like one of them, and I realized how I didn't miss it at all. There had been more hustle and bustle in my day as a college student and less fun then I remember, but it had paid off, and a tax-paying adult had far more freedom then the young nineteen-year-old lady still living at home that had first graced that campus. I thought about Katie suddenly in that moment. As young as I had been, without the fall back of parents…what had been her fall back? It was easy to assume that James had easily become her whole world. What about her own parents, her family, her friends? More questions to answer, more searching before me. I stepped through the front door—solid wood and hand-carved, they were a spectacular addition. A large tile lobby with fake plants and art deco furniture greeted me. The registration desk was far less helpful.

"I'm sorry, I'm not privileged to give out any information on a former student even if deceased."

"Not to the cops either?" I interjected.

The bright young woman on the other side of the counter looked at me like I was trouble. "Are you the police?"

I sighed and shook my head.

"Feel free to tour the campus, Miss Black, and if you have any further questions about admittance, I can set you up with a counselor."

I thanked her anyway and turned to go, seeing if I could at least figure out where Mrs. Whitaker's class was on such a large campus. I became so engrossed in my own thoughts I failed to see him until we collided.

"Oh gosh, I'm so sorry. Here, let me help."

It was almost as if he expected this as daily routine, as I stooped to help him pick up the papers. An older gentleman well into his fifties or sixties by my guess, his hairline receding from a soft yet handsome face framed by brown glasses. He wore a button-up blue shirt and dark-blue tie and brown slacks. I pegged him for a professor but got the surprise of my life.

"Thank you. No worries."

He offered me a quick polite smile and scurried around the corner. I watched him disappear behind an office door that read Counseling. I quickly followed.

The single wood door opened to a reception area with a row of gray hardbacked chairs that faced a matching counter. A young blond-haired woman who looked just out of her teens sat behind a computer screen, red lacquered nails typing away. She paused and looked up at me and smiled right on cue.

"Can I help you?"

This time, I threw my title around, doing nothing to impress the young woman, but I managed to grab her attention anyways.

"I'm inquiring about a former student, Katie Pearson."

"Do you know who her counselor was? I can see whether he or she is available for you to speak with. I take it you don't have an appointment?"

The eyebrows arched.

"No, but I know whom I was here to speak with. Gary Allen."

"Dr. Allen. Yes, one moment."

She pivoted the chair around and got up, smoothing a deep navy-blue sleeveless dress over ample hips and tottered back behind a temporary wall on short, chunky heels. She reappeared a moment later with the same man I had run smack into in the hallway. It was his turn to look bewildered.

"I'm Dr. Allen. Did I miss something?"

I was assuming that he meant I knew his name by the fact he had dropped something else in our collision that he had missed.

"Listen. I just need five minutes of your time."

I offered my best smile, hoping he would take it. I was stretching pretty far at that point. He checked his wristwatch.

"I guess I can spare five minutes. Sure, come on back, um…"

"Michael."

I followed him back past a couple cubicles to his desk.

"So what can I help you with?"

I sat down and crossed my hands in my lap.

"Listen, I'm not sure you can help me at all. I'm looking for an old friend. She attended school here."

"Well, you're right about that. Any information she gave to any of our counselors or her records are personal, and you know I can't divulge that information to you."

I sighed. "I'm a therapist. I get the patient-client confidentiality thing."

He looked at me, a bit bewildered.

"If you're not applying for admission to state or currently a student, I feel like you're wasting your time."

*You're telling me*, I thought. Instead I blurted out the name. "Katie Pearson…"

I expected a quick answer. Instead, I got a pause, and a look flickered across his gaze.

"I can't tell you one way or the other. You can go to admissions. They can let you know the time frame she attended, perhaps a current address. That's all I can offer you. Now please, I have actual appointments to attend to."

I got up, paused, and pivoted.

"One last question. Did Katie ever see a counselor for anything other than academic counseling?"

I let the question linger in the air.

He paused, rifled through some papers. "You know I can't answer that."

I pressed ahead, feeling I might be kicked out before I had a chance to finish my next question. "But you offer mental health counseling?"

Long frustrated sigh. "Yes, we do, and I myself in particular do, but that is beside the question. I will not answer that. Now please… before I call security…"

He didn't even get up to show me out. He pointed down the hall. I left musing over his odd answers. If Katie had never received any counseling, wouldn't it have been easy to just say no? Since Admissions had been so kind in the first place to answer any of my questions, I wandered back out on the campus. I stopped the first student I ran into and asked where Mrs. Whitaker's class was.

I could hear the professor's voice echoing into the hall as I approached the door of English lit. I checked my watch and then opened the door, slipping into the auditorium mostly undetected except for a row of students in the far back. I offered an apologetic smile and stole an empty seat. It took thirty more minutes for the lecture to end. I got up and made my way through the sea of students rushing off to their next class. Nostalgia and my old days hit me. A tall, well-built woman with a slight Arizona tan and thick, wavy brownish-gray hair dressed in a turquoise silk top and pressed slacks stood with her back to me, going through some papers at a nearby desk. She turned at my interruption.

"Yes?"

Her eyebrows arched. She probably assumed I was a student, but she was probably perplexed by her lack of memory of me.

"Michael."

I offered; she shook my hand.

"I don't—"

"I'm not in your class yet. An old friend, Katie, Katie Pearson, took some classes here. I'm trying to locate her. Someone said she took a creative writing course you taught perhaps a few years back…"

Mrs. Whitaker smiled.

"I teach hundreds of students a day. I'm not sure I could remember one single…"

I pulled the engagement photo out, and she took a long moment to study the petite blonde in the photo, and her face changed. Already creased lines seemed to stretch more as she handed the photo back.

"Actually, the police were here a few weeks ago. You're not associated with them, are you?" she asked hesitantly, perhaps trying to poke holes in my story.

"No, really, I'm—"

"Between the police and now you, she must be in some sort of trouble, though I can't imagine what."

"So you do remember her?"

"Yes, her I do remember. I would like to say I remember all my students, but that's impossible. She was an eager one, always came early to get a spot up front, always taking notes and asking questions. She was very intelligent, very serious and studious…"

The door opened, and more students began to fill the isles.

"Listen, I have another class in about ten minutes, but if you can come back, my last class is at four."

"Sure, that would be great."

I walked away and into the warm Arizona sunshine. As enjoyable as it was for the moment, I couldn't imagine the heat index in the summer. Strolling across the campus and back toward my car, I figured the best thing to fill my time till then was to do a little more research. Time to investigate the second address for Miss Katie Pearson.

## Chapter 21

I was far from alone though and not the only one to arrive in the warm Arizona sunshine. Katie idled along the street, watching me pull out of the university parking lot. Katie had borne witness to more than I knew, and she had worked effortlessly to piece her shattered life back together more than once. No one had stopped her then, and no one was going to stop her know.

"You just don't know when to call it quits…" Katie murmured under her breath as my car sped past her, and back on the open road, Katie flipped a U turn and followed a few car lengths behind. Just outside the hustle and bustle of downtown Tempe, the highway bled out into the open, deserted dessert and low-lying foothills before it crashed into private, well-appointed neighborhoods. Katie kept her distance, falling back as the road opened up, and she had nothing but a single semi between her and me. Katie's heart hummed in her chest and her breath caught in her throat as she followed me out to the old neighborhood. It had been a long time since she had cruised out this way, and she felt every inch of terror and anxiety she had left behind in this place.

All Katie's secrets, all her childhood, was behind the stucco walls and tiled roof of that elegant mini estate her parents had once upon a time called home. Katie paused at the entrance to the neighborhood, watching me melt away into the scenery. She didn't need anyone to guide her; she could find the house with her eyes closed.

"If you had any idea, Michael. If you only knew."

Rage boiled inside Katie's blood, and she gripped the steering wheel hard with her fingers. Her careful, well-executed plan crumbled before her. She had one more loose end to tie up.

## Chapter 22

Flagstaff was a smaller, more urban city roughly a two-hour drive on highway forty, which traversed caravans of open, rocky dessert unpopulated by much other than wildlife. Katie's birthplace and the city she had roamed until she was old enough to leave, as my presumptions led me to believe. Just north of the town was Gray Mountain, an unincorporated community in Coconino County.

Katie Pearson's childhood home sat behind the iron gates of a private estate in Gray Mountain's rolling hills. It sat on a manufactured grass; small glasslike pools of water shimmered, and palm trees caught a soft breeze. The houses were surrounded by a private golf course, and each house's backyard opened to the putting ground. I took a few rights and lefts away from pastel and brown two- and three-story small sprawling estates that looked like they had been built in the last decade to the older, more original part of the neighborhood. Set in the back, away from the putting green, it faced out into the Arizona dessert. I slowed down and scanned the house numbers till I found what I was looking for: two stories of cream-colored stucco and a burnt-orange tiled roof. It looked like it fit in an Italian vineyard; it was total Tuscany style, and I loved its sprawling glory immediately.

I pulled up to a wrought-iron gate covered by lush small shrubs and tropical flowers. I could see the expansive green front lawn and more of the same plant combinations. A long drive in the shape of a horseshoe snaked away from the heavy locked gate, and I noted the fragrance of the orange and lemon trees along the way. I parked my car near the gate and walked up to the call box, unsure of what answers, if any, I would find here. I had no idea of Katie's association to this house or whom I would find inside. I pressed the button on the call box and let it buzz anyway.

A thick, soft Spanish accent crackled out, "*Si*...may I help you?"

I pushed the button to answer. "Is this the owner of the home?"

"*Porvo*, no sales *porvo*..."

The line went dead. I paused for a brief moment and pushed the button back. "No sales. I just had a few questions about the previous owner. She was an old friend of mine."

I waited a moment, and another voice crackled across the line, no accent, soft and feminine.

"This is Olivia. I'm the current owner. May I help you?"

"I am looking for an old friend. This was her listed address."

I expected a quick answer and to be on my way, but to my surprise, the gate began to open.

"Please come in."

I headed up the drive heavily shaded by the fruit bushes, their blossoms not producing fruit at this time but still leaving a fragrance in the air. Olivia met me at the front stoop. She was a short deep-brown-skinned woman I guessed of Hispanic descent. The long, form-fitting white sleeveless dress that went to her ankles showed off her curves nicely. Long brownish-red hair was pinned back from an oval face with large dark eyes; red lips smiled invitingly at me.

"Please..."

She stepped back as I approached and led me through a large wood door into a cool tile entry in shades of browns oranges and blues. The ceiling shot up to the second floor; it was expansive and made the house feel regal. I wondered about Katies association to this abode, if any.

"You have a lovely home."

Olivia smiled. "Thank you."

I followed her into a room to the left. The sofa and chairs were pure white. China hutches with glass doors showed off beautiful pieces of stone pottery in bright hues, and gold-colored frames housed large paintings of flowers. Lightly tinted yellow walls and heavy, thick blue drapes made up the remainder of the room. I sat down on one of two small stark white loveseats that faced each other. Another woman dressed in a black short-sleeved uniform and white apron came into the room with a silver carafe of coffee and a tray filled with cups of cream and sugar. After the triple mocha, my heart rate was doing fine, but I wasn't one to be impolite and allowed the woman to pour me a cup. The pair of ladies spoke softly in Spanish to one another before the woman in the black dress disappeared into what I assumed was the kitchen. I took the offered cup and splashed in a bit of cream. The flavors burst on my tongue; it was dark and rich and sweet all at once.

"Delicious."

Olivia smiled. "Thank you. My husband and I, we brew it ourselves. We own a coffee shop in Flagstaff, good business. We have had our ups and downs, but right now, things are good."

Her eyes roamed the walls of the room. I smiled encouragingly.

"How long have you owned this house?"

"About three years, going on four…"

I did the math as quickly as I could in my head. Close to four years would put her back around when she met James, so it must have been when she had pulled ship, so to speak, and rented the apartment.

"Whom were you looking for?"

"A Katie, Katie Pearson."

By reasonable deduction, I assumed there was no relation. Olivia nodded.

"Oh yes. Nice gal. Sold us this property at a good price. We were very surprised. We thought there was no way we would get it. She literally asked us what we were willing to pay. We kind of laughed it off. She just seemed in a hurry. It had been on the market a week when we looked at it—probably the third person to look at it. We threw her a number we thought she would laugh at, and she said yes. She said she didn't need the money. I guess she had lost her parents and then her aunt. Poor girl, she just didn't want the memory, I guess. Somehow the aunt or someone in her family had paid it off, so everything she made minus the real estate fees was all profit."

Olivia paused and looked around.

"Such a big, gorgeous house, though. We are grateful."

I nodded in agreement and sipped more of the fragrant coffee.

"So you're an old friend?"

I nodded, sticking with my original story.

"Yes, lost contact with her, just kind of checking in where she was last."

Olivia shrugged. "I wish I could help you, but other than that meeting, we dealt strictly with the real estate agent. We never dealt with her directly. She did say she was moving closer to Arizona state. Guess she was attending college there. They might have some info. Such a great girl."

Same old story. I finished the coffee out of politeness.

"Thank you. I'll check with them, and thank you for your time."

"Of course. I'm sorry I couldn't have been of more help. One moment."

As we stood up, she disappeared for a moment into the kitchen and returned with a small silver bag with a business card clipped to it.

"For your troubles. Enjoy please."

I nodded thanks and wondered if this had turned into a sales call, nonetheless on her part and not mine. I sniffed the fragrances of the yard under the crisp, blue sky one last time. As I headed down the drive to my car, the gate clicked open just as I got there, and I offered Olivia a quick wave before climbing in my car. As I drove away, I thought about the bridge between the past and the future and how one so greatly affected the other. No matter how great the passage of time, some things are never forgotten and manifest themselves in different ways. They intertwine so deeply with one's soul that in the end, they make or break who they are. Katie's past had been speckled by death. The deep pain of loss could never be taken lightly, and the fact that one just got over it and moved on was unreasonable to assume. Learning that she had suffered such a great loss in her young life, I could only imagine, as a therapist and a person, what impact the death of her parents had on Katie as a young girl and then to lose her aunt. Whether their relationship had been good or not was beside the point—a loss was a loss. I checked my clock on the dash of the car and realized I had just enough time minus any traffic to make it back to the university.

## Chapter 23

Mrs. Whitaker met me in the college cafeteria. We sat in the far back by tall glass windows that glinted at the dessert hues and the building around us. A few students milled about, most likely for the night classes and lectures offered, but things were shutting down slowly.

"What would you like to know?"

She stirred a couple sugar packets into some iced tea.

"I actually grew up in the South, Georgia area to be exact. Still can't take the sweet tea out of me, and no one makes it right around here."

I smiled.

"I can imagine. Anyway, thanks again for meeting me, Mrs. …"

She shrugged and sipped the tea.

"It's hardly a Mrs. anymore. All that's waiting for me at home are a pile of papers to grade and a couple of cats. George, my husband—he writes and travels around to lecture. He's gone half the year, and kids, well, we were never blessed with those…"

She prattled on about life for a moment.

"Sorry, enough about me."

"How well did you know Katie?" I asked and she shrugged again.

"As well as any other student. She never let on about her private life. Some students seemed to divulge that information but not Katie. We did a few creative writing pieces on family, but she never had much to say. She always stuck out as a bit odd to me, kinda closed off, but she was always wanting to do her best. Got straight As."

I offered the information I had gathered.

"Yes, her parents passed away when she was little, a very unfortunate thing." Mrs. Whitaker nodded. "We met after class one day when she having a hard time on a family piece. She explained that her parents were gone, and I guess the aunt raising her was too. It was just her. I encouraged her to write about something that was important to her instead of something personal, even from her past of what she remembered."

"Do you remember, if anything, what she wrote?"

She shook her head. "Her writing was always very good, though—poignant and elegant and well-thought-out. I guess she said her intent was to go to law school. She wanted to be a defense attorney. Isn't that ironic? Now the police are after her. I can't believe they said they were investigating the death of her ex-fiancé. Never even knew she was engaged, but my students' personal life is not mine to inquire on."

"Felt she could have done something else."

Mrs. Whitaker shrugged. "She was very smart. I think she could have done anything. She didn't strike me as a person who knew her own worth, ya know…" She looked at me for a second. "Well, you two were friends. I'm sure you know what I'm talking about."

I nodded in agreement, though I didn't have a clue. "Is there anything else significant you can tell me about her?"

Mrs. Whitaker took me in for a second as if analyzing me. "You ask more questions than the police. What's your real interest in here?"

I sighed. Being a detective was not in my cards if I couldn't remain covert. "I care about her and her well-being—that's all I can say. I have a vested personal interest in the outcome of this case. I can't say any more than that."

Long pause a few nail taps on the table. "I really can't say more. I didn't know her all that well either. She seemed a bright, creative girl with a future in front of her. Now if you don't mind, I have a stack of papers to go home to and a couple of cats that are probably getting restless for their dinner."

We shook hands, and I politely thanked her for her time. As I watched her leave for a second, I knew I still had a lot of work ahead of me. I headed back to my car and crossed town in the settling dusk to my hotel room. I thought about love in that moment, how love could conquer, how love could divide, how love did so many wonderful things but how love could also turn into something more catastrophic. I thought of the one great love of my life that had driven me to succeed in more ways than one. The heartache that was had pushed me forward into the life I had currently made for myself, into a career that was flourishing but a personal life that was neglected and falling apart. Katie had been just as driven for different reasons. Her pain had not come from heartache but the heartbreak of losing her only parents and then the only family member she had left until she was literally and completely alone in this world. It wasn't about the money. It wasn't about the age difference. It struck me then like a lightbulb going off, and I wondered why I hadn't seen it before. It was about family. It was about James becoming her entire world until he was so much a part of her she couldn't imagine being without him. When James had broken their engagement, he had done more than break her heart; he had uprooted her and taken everything from her, leaving her completely alone and disconnected in this world. Still, it seemed so useless, so wasteful for Katie to think of the foolish notion that if she couldn't have James then no one could. In the end, losing James was debilitating. It brought forth all of her past all at once, slamming into her like an entire ocean, and everything inside of Katie exploded at once. Dusk had begun to settle in brilliant neon shades of pinks and oranges on the horizon as I made my way back to my hotel room, my mind loaded with a million questions and my body physically weary from trekking around town. My stomach joined the party and began to growl as I parked the car near the front lobby and made my way inside. Nothing satisfies hunger on so many levels like cookies, and even though it was a bad decision, I couldn't help but snag two from the overflowing plate on the concierge counter.

"Thanks," I mumbled, offering a smile at the clerk and fishing out my room key from my pocket. I headed down the hall, past a wall of windows that offered a view of an indoor pool. Kids splashed and squalled, and parents lingered nearby. The hot tub looked inviting, but I figured maybe after bedtime hours when things were a bit quieter. I had polished off one cookie and was working on the second as I unlocked my door and headed inside. The air was cool almost too cool for my taste. I padded past the bathroom to the knob on the wall that controlled the fan and adjusted the temp a tad more to my liking before tossing myself back across the freshly made bed. I lay like that for a brief moment, polished off the cookie, and began to think about what to grab for dinner when my phone began to vibrate. I picked it up and checked the incoming number on the glowing screen. I was pleasantly surprised as I answered, "Hey, stranger."

Soft, husky chuckle. I suddenly found myself switching gears from thinking about Katie's love life to my own.

"Hi. Hope you don't mind my calling. I just…"

I peeled myself off the bed and kicked off my shoes, pacing the floor like a nervous teenager. I hated the way this man could still leave me so undone even though I had sworn up and down the moment he left town that we would never be more than friends because it was all too complicated.

"No, of course not. I take it you're settled at home?"

I heard unfamiliar noises in the background and suddenly tried to imagine what he was doing, what home was like.

"Yes. Flight was good. Nice to be back to work, in a routine, I guess you could say…"

We chatted until the room was so dark I had to switch on a lamp. We talked about work and other pleasantries. Time rushed by in a hurry, and minutes swiftly turned into an hour.

"Anyway, I should let you go. I'm sure you have more important things going on than talking to me."

I was sitting on the bed, my legs crisscrossed. The line had beeped twice in the midst of our conversation, and I knew I should check to see who it was. The clock on the nightstand nearby read a quarter to seven.

"More important than talking to you? Never."

We shared a soft, flirtatious laugh, and I suddenly found myself on uneven territory.

"I'll give you a call soon."

There was that awkward silence for a split second where neither one of us knew how to say goodbye. Flashes of all our teenage conversations when the longing had been real flitted through my mind for the briefest of seconds, and then finally, we simply said goodbye and mutually clicked the End buttons on our phones. I scrolled through the missed calls and was not surprised to see not only had Maria phoned but so had Richard. I checked the voicemail and found Richard had left a long one. I read the text from it and gathered it wasn't much more than a hello and where the hell I was. I made a mental note to call him later perhaps and dialed Maria instead.

"Hey, girl, you're still alive."

I laughed. "Very funny."

"Find what you were looking for?"

"In a way. I learned a lot about Katie. Seems odd, really. Everyone seemed to like her. Even I like her the more I get to know her. You even feel sorry for her in a way."

I relayed the information about her aunt and her parents, the house, the apartment—everything I had learned and then some.

"Sounds like she had her own money?"

"Yes, doesn't sound like she was hurting financially, and she was driven, had a good head on her shoulders. Smart, financially set, young, and headstrong. She was James's equal. Maybe it was too much of a good thing?"

Maria offered another vantage point. "Maybe it wasn't James hiding something—maybe it was her. Doesn't sound like anyone really had much to say about her."

I thought about that, how Katie had been painted as a smart, creative, quiet, non-social girl, but something had to be beyond the façade. No one was made up of nothing. Try as we might, we all came from somewhere; we all had a past.

"Maybe a little more digging is necessary…"

Maria yawned almost a little to dramatically across the line.

"Okay, say no more. Go get some shut-eye."

"Do me a favor, though."

"Yeah, say no more. I'll see what I can find out on my end about the lovely couple who produced Miss Katie Pearson."

We shared a friendly laugh, and then the line went dead. I gazed at the phone for a minute. My thoughts turned a mile a minute in my head, but my stomach began to cramp taking precedence over all other matters. I contemplated the massive amount of caffeine I had had that day. I wasn't sure if food had played a part at all. I mused over getting back in my car and settling for fast food or staying in the comfort of my hotel room and ordering out. I threw some food searches into my phone and settled on Chinese. After placing an order of steamed veggies and some sort of spicy chicken dish and a side of rice, I pulled out my laptop and sat cross-legged on the bed. Time to have a little fun with Google. As before, web searches didn't bring up much, and if Katie had a Facebook, Instagram, or any other social media page, it was buried under a pseudonym that might take me years to figure out.

"No one comes from nothing...."

I talked to myself out loud; my fingers stayed poised over the keyboard. I had never had a reason to delve into Katie's past until that moment. If her aunt and her parents were deceased, it was all I could do to know about them. I realized I had no idea how old Katie was when she had lost her parents and knew that could mean any number of things, but knowing they had both been relatively young, I searched the online community of Flagstaff, Arizona, using the house's address and the name *Pearson* to see what I could draw from the worldwide web. I assumed their passing had been together, and I knew that had to point to some sort of tragic accident, and I was right on cue. The AZL paper's online version popped up *Pearson* in relation to an article printed in 2008 when Katie, I surmised, would have been a twelve-year-old girl. What I read startled me:

    A young couple dead after an apparent house invasion.

> Mr. and Mrs. Pearson were discovered shot to death in their home. They are survived by two young girls, Katie and Patricia, 12 and 14…

I hurriedly scanned the article. I had no inclination until that moment that Katie had a sister, and I wondered if that was the secret that had wrecked her perfectly crafted world. I continued flipping through several papers for the entire month, looking for any other relevance to the case until I found what I was looking for right there in black and white:

> Patricia Pearson, the couple's older daughter, was found guilty of the murders of her parents due to her mental instability. She was sent to a psychiatric facility…

I jumped as a loud knock sounded on the door. Sighing and trying to still my racing heart, I laughed at the idiocy and grabbed my wallet, padding to the door. I opened it and collected my late supper, gave a decent tip, and headed back to the bed. I took my laptop to the desk and chowed down on fresh chunks of broccoli steamed rice and chicken that was just the right kind of spicy as I scrolled through the remainder of the paper, as hungry physically as I was mentally.

## Chapter 24

The next morning, I found myself at the one place that might answer more of my questions in greater detail than Google, the Flagstaff Police Department. I wanted to believe Katie was virtuous in her efforts, but I couldn't help believe that she had something more to do with her parents' outcome then the papers were letting on. I wondered as well if Patricia and her parents' death had been the secret that Katie had tried to keep to herself, crafting such an elaborate illusion that when James found out, it was all she could do to explode in a fiery rage.

"Sorry, I can't offer you anything better."

He smiled and offered me a hot cup of what looked like black mud, but I was grateful for more caffeine.

"I appreciate your time, Lieutenant."

I sipped the concoction at hand as he sat down across from me on the other side of the long lacquered wood desk, a small office that faced out to a dozen or so cubicles. Lieutenant Greg Marshal was in charge of the Homicide division.

"Don't thank me. Thank Maria. She is just a rookie, but I have a feeling that girl will go far in this business."

Greg sat down behind the long lacquered wood desk, his name in brass surrounded by a few glass picture frames of what I assumed were his wife and children. He was a tall, well-built man with soft brown hair and matching eyes. With the timeline, he was probably well into his forties.

"That's my daughter Lily. She's practically a graduating senior now. She was in grade school then during the case you're inquiring about. I wasn't much farther than your friend Maria. I wasn't the investigator on the case. I was on patrol that night, helped keep chaos down on the scene, so to speak."

He pulled out a thin file and laid it on the desk.

"Everything you need to know is in here, but it was a pretty cut-and-dry case."

Greg clicked his tongue and shook his head.

"Will never forget it. Those two little girls just standing there, parents both dead just a few feet away…but the truth of the matter—that was even worse."

Greg tapped the file and shoved it in my direction. I put my hand on it and paused.

"Yes, I found out Katie had a sister. That wasn't apparently public knowledge. Was it always like that in the family?"

"What, Patricia?"

Greg leaned back in his chair and took a long second, almost as if he was walking back inside in a forgotten memory.

"Patricia was different. A lot of people knew the family well because of her. Had a few calls out that way, started about two years before the murder. Patricia was schizophrenic and had what they called episodes, but none of it got really bad until she hit the teens and flat out refused to stop taking her meds. I followed a few calls, and it was always the same old story. She would go to the hospital, they would stabilize her, she would get better, return home, and get rebellious again."

I flipped open the file and began to scan the information at hand.

"Patricia was found guilty?"

"Yes. At first, we didn't know what happened. We thought someone broke into the home. They were the nicest couple, but you learn in this business and perhaps a little bit in yours, looks can be deceiving. People hide all kinds of stuff."

I nodded in agreement. "It says here no murder weapon was found, yet they were both shot fatally?" I looked up.

"There wasn't much of a formal investigation done. One girl, Katie, ratted the other one out shortly after, and Patricia didn't deny it."

"Did she confess?"

Our eyes met.

"So it was Katie's word against Patricia's?"

"It made the most sense at the time. It wasn't like Patricia hadn't been violent in the past. We had a record of calls made, and some of them were for physical violence against her parents at times."

I sighed as my eyes scanned the glossy five-by-seven photos of the young deceased couple and closed it up, shoving it back in the lieutenant's direction.

"Listen, you may be in the business of facts, but I'm in the business of knowing why, the reason behind the madness, if you will."

He smiled.

"I think you know as well as I do that sometimes people can snap. I may have been a rookie kid at the time and had my doubts, but it's been quite a few years since then."

It was my turn to reflect, but something beyond my capacity as a therapist tore at the back of my mind.

"So you believe to tell me that two young girls got up one day and conspired to kill their parents?"

Greg looked at me in overwhelming frustration.

"I believe one girl was off her meds and had a psychotic break and snapped if you want my opinion."

I didn't like his opinion at all.

"I have seen people with different mental illness snap and fly into a rage."

I grabbed the folder back and snapped it open, pointing to the photo of the couple lying face down on the cold tiles of their house.

"They were both shot in the back of the head, meaning they were unsuspecting. Someone had snuck up on them. That seems very calculated to me, do you not agree? What about the weapon? Someone had the forethought to carefully hide that as well! None of that adds up, and you as well as I know that. So what I think is you were very eager to see me because you have wanted a reason to reopen this case but never had any authority until now."

He counteracted my theory at that.

"Well, I'll give you a maybe."

I looked at him, knowing we could battle our sides back and forth, but all I knew of Katie led me to believe differently. If there was a secret worth killing for, it was murder.

"I have evidence to believe otherwise, and I think you know in your heart of hearts what the truth is, and I think that has stuck with you. She was the smarter of the two, wasn't she? Even at twelve, she acted like an adult…"

Greg sighed, swiveled the chair a bit, and drummed his fingertips thoughtfully on the desktop.

"She had her head hanging. Her hair was in her face. She looked like she had been crying. Patricia, that was…"

"Katie?"

"Katie, she was just standing there emotionless. I remember her looking directly at me. Someone from the county led the girls away. It bothered me when I learned of the confession. I questioned it myself. It seemed to make no sense, but they were eager to close it—small town and all that. They took what they had and ran."

Katie ran too, I thought idly. She took the money and ran figuratively. Everything had been left to her, and as she grew from a child into a woman, she thought she had neatly buried the past until someone came along and discovered the skeleton in her closet, and the trail I knew started with Patricia.

"Where is Patricia know?"

"Long-term psychiatric hospital, last time I checked."

"Whom did the care of Katie go to?"

"Her aunt, of course, only other living relative or one willing to take her. She was an older gal, though—well into her late sixties by then. She passed away from cancer, I believe, when Katie was just nineteen. That girl was in the midst of one tragedy after another."

I looked right at him and asked the most pressing question. "Do you think she was innocent?"

He shook his head.

"Facts are the only thing that speak in this business. I can't say one way or the other."

I thanked him for his time and headed back out. I idled my car in the shade of a palm tree and dialed in the number of the Arizona

State Mental Hospital. It took a little maneuvering through the phone system and the staff till I reached the appropriate person. A little more smooth talking and a few of my credentials and some names thrown around, and I had myself a makeshift appointment in a couple hours.

## Chapter 25

With time to kill and my mind going at a hundred-plus miles an hour, I circled around the downtown area of Flagstaff, Arizona, looking for a coffee shop or someplace I could log in and power up both my computer and myself. Settling on a small sandwich shop that looked inviting, I took the time to feed my physical self as well as my mental. I was not surprised to find halfway through a toasted ham and cheese that both girls had attended a private Catholic school in the area—and not just any but one of the oldest and reputable schools. San Francisco De Asis was originally founded in 1889, making it the oldest school in Flagstaff and the next stop on my list.

The school was framed and redesigned with large lacquered wood beams and brown stone. It was a relic and well-preserved through the course of time. It was a definite beauty against the backdrop of the Arizona desert. As I pulled into the school parking lot and headed up to the front door, I mused over what I might say to slide past the administration area. Copies of yearbooks online had given me a list of several of Katie's teachers in the twelve grades she had traversed the halls of this school, and I figured with dumb luck, someone between her fourth and twelve year would still be teaching. I took a stab at the first name, somewhere in the middle.

Mrs. Ames was in her midforties, a short woman with frosted blond hair and a warm smile and a pumpkin-orange blouse under a gray blazer that matched her pressed slacks. She paced the front of the room, pointing out items on the smart board the way you would on a chalkboard. She was just old enough to come from a different generation when such a thing was still in style. I waited for a bell to ring and the fourth graders pile out of lunch. A sea of skirts and slacks and wrinkle-free blouses.

"Mrs. Ames?"

She looked at me and smiled and scanned me quickly. I tapped my chest just where the visitor's badge was plastered.

"Come on, um…"

"Michael," I offered, following her into a well-appointed and decorated classroom.

"How can I help you today?"

She sat down behind her desk and offered me a student chair. I took a seat.

"You were Katie Pearson's fifth grade teacher many years ago. I came inquiring about her for, um, police matters…"

Her face turned an ash-gray color as if she had seen a ghost and her hand went for her chest. For a split second, I thought she might faint. Slowly the color rushed back to her cheeks, and she made a soft coughing noise.

"Oh my goodness. I haven't thought about that girl in ages, but yes…yes, I remember her well, actually."

Another coughing sound, and this time, she fished out a small bag from her desk.

"If you don't mind, I didn't have much breakfast."

She opened the bag, and I motioned for her to continue. After taking a moment to rummage around for a fork, she opened the lid to what appeared to be some sort of leafy green salad. She took small, delicate bites.

"Can I ask why you're here? You said it was for the police?"

I bit my lip and pressed forward. "Nothing I can really speak about—just reason to believe she may be involved in a specific matter."

Mrs. Ames didn't look like she was buying what I was selling but didn't seem to mind walking down memory lane. In fact, a small smile crept up on her lips.

"I can't really tell you anything that might be of relevance. She was a very smart girl, quiet, kept to herself a lot but always eager to learn, always kind to others. I just…she was so shy. That's how she stuck with me—like a flower that wouldn't open all the way."

"Can you tell me anything about her home life?"

Mrs. Ames took more bites and made a quick wipe of her mouth with a napkin.

"They always came in together. Saw them a couple times for conferences, but that was it. Katie made good grades, wasn't a troublemaker at all that I knew of. She didn't seem to like any attention drawn to her, good or bad."

I pushed forward. "What about her sister, Patricia?"

"Oh well. Her I remember. Just a grade or two above Katie. The school seemed to know her all too well, but she was a sweet child too. She just, well, she had issues, ya know…"

She looked at me for confirmation.

"I heard she was schizophrenic."

"Yes, that's what she was diagnosed with eventually. She was here through her early years, but when she hit high school, she was sent away to another school, a school more equipped to fit her needs."

Right about the time her parents had expired, I thought.

"Of course that was right after the…um…that was such a tragedy. Her parents…if Katie was quiet before, she was stone silent then."

I nodded as I listened.

"So Katie continued to go to school here till she graduated and Patricia got sent away?"

Mrs. Ames struggled for a moment with her words, and a tear suddenly leapt out of her hazel eyes. She wiped it away quickly. "If you work with the police, Michael, you should know what happened to her parents. I'm sorry, but I don't wish to talk about that. It was so awful."

*If only you knew*, I thought to myself.

"I'm sorry. Was there anything else you can tell me about either girl?"

The salad suddenly got closed up and disappeared inside its bag. Looked like I had touched a real soft spot.

"No, not really. Katie was quite even more quiet and withdrawn after that, um, event, but she was always got good grades, was always kind to others. Patricia was always out to cause trouble but seemed to get away with a lot because I think those that worked with her knew it wasn't her fault, in her control I mean."

I tried one last angle.

"How were the kids toward her?"

Mrs. Ames shrugged her shoulders.

"As kids could be. A lot just ignored her, and some…some could be a bit cruel, I suppose."

"Did she have any friends?"

"Not really. I never saw her hanging out with any one in particular around here at least."

The bell gave a sudden sharp ring.

"Listen they will be through the door momentarily, so…"

"Are any of Katie's other teachers still working here?"

"No, a lot of the elders retired, sorry to say."

We were interrupted by noisy footfalls and loud chatter. The door swung open, and Mrs. Ames got up, creating order, as I left in the midst of chaos. As I headed back to my car and for the next stop on my list, a picture was slowly being painted of a fragile girl who had perhaps been pushed a little too far.

## Chapter 26

Arizona State Mental Hospital had been originally erected in the 1800s as an insane asylum. Several centuries later, it had softened and was now a long-term psychiatric hospital for those that were a threat to themselves or others and tried to implement a community feel and more human approach. A flat white several-story structure in Phoenix, a short twenty-minute commute from my hotel in Tempe, it wasn't that far at all from Katie and where she had grown up. I parked in the visitor parking and headed up to the front doors of the hospital armed with the authority of a mental health professional. I was hoping it would allow me some free access, but I was limited in my world.

The hospital was bisected by units depending upon the patients' needs or what translated as their level of security and safety for themselves and the staff members. Patricia was housed in a long-term wing where patients stayed for months or years as long as the bills were paid and someone was paying Patricia's bills, and I had a little idea of just whom was footing the bill. Patricia's floor was for low security risk patients. I pushed the call button and was escorted through two double doors and stopped directly at the nurses' station. The remainder of the wing was a group of common day rooms and halls of shared and private rooms.

"Ah, Michael. Call me Megan please."

A woman with kinky black hair braided back against a plain face without makeup, dressed in a long multi-patterned skirt and flowing green blouse. Her handshake was firm and strong.

"Thank you for meeting with me."

Megan was one of the lead nurses and coordinators for the floor. She led me away from the desk and down the first hall to the left.

"We have a few private rooms. Patricia is in one of them. Sometimes it's for the needs of the patient, sometimes it's by request. This time, it's a little of both. She is quite tired this morning."

The door was open, and light from a window filtered across yellow-tinged linoleum floors and splashed across a single twin bed with an aqua blue and pink quilted blanket. It was the only sense of home in this place. The walls were bare and beige. A desk and a bookcase were the only other occupants. A few well-worn paperbacks and a variety of soft trinkets helped add a sense of home to the place. Patricia favored her sister, a little heavier in the body. Her frame was shapeless in dark gray scrubs, her hair a few shades darker than Katie's was in a rumpled state against her smooth, rosy skin. Listless blue eyes stared off into space, and she rocked back and forth on the bed.

"As you can see, she had a long night. I'm not sure she will be up for talking. She doesn't have as many psychotic breaks as she used to, but she has her moments."

The nurse stood with me in the doorway to Patricia's room.

"I'll be at the station. Leave the door open and call if you need me."

I approached softly.

"Patricia..."

The rocking momentarily stopped, and the blue eyes with the long lashes looked at me. She was a striking young girl, just as pretty as her sister even on a bad day.

"Can we talk? My name's Michael..."

I paused and stepped closer to the bed. She backed up protectively and tucked her knees to her chest.

"It's okay. I'm here about your sister."

Double blinks and lip movement and then something flashed across her eyes. I wondered if she even remembered her sister, if Katie even visited her.

"My sister...Katie?"

I nodded and took a seat on the end of the bed.

Patricia gripped her head and let out a long growl. She suddenly leapt up off the bed and began to pace, twirling her fingers in her blond locks. I wondered momentarily as a professional if coming back on a better day mood-wise would be best.

"I don't want to talk about her—she's a bad girl, a very bad girl."

I opened my mouth to speak, but Patricia snapped.

"My head hurts. They gave me pills. I guess I was a bad girl last night."

Midtwenties, but she developmentally acted a lot younger. By her actions alone, I knew there was more to her diagnosis.

"A bad girl like Katie?"

She leapt forward toward me.

"She is not my sister!" Patricia snapped, and I saw fluid lucidity flow back.

"Why is she not your sister?"

Patricia looked at me. Anger flushed her cheeks. "She took them!"

"Took who?"

Another frustrated emotional sigh.

"Mom and Dad. She took them, and now I'm here. I'm here all the time, and she…she is out there!"

Patricia gripped her hair and tugged and then pointed out the window.

"She killed them, Patricia?"

Sudden tears sprung forth.

"Yes, not Patricia, not like they say, but Katie…Katie did it. She said…she said if I told, they would put her away for life. She said if I said I did it, they would be…"

"They would be kinder because of your mind, the way you think?"

Patricia nodded.

"But now I'm here and they won't let me leave ever, and Katie is out there and…and…why? Why did she kill them?"

A torrent of sobs erupted from Patricia, and she tucked her face against her knees. I didn't need to call for the nurse. I heard the shuffle and squeak of the nurse's shoes coming down the hall, and I got up and began to retreat from the room.

"Wait!"

The nurse paused in the doorway ready to charge in, when Patricia stopped crying and looked up, pushing her hair back from her face.

"Yes?"

I stepped forward but allowed her her space.

"In the house? In Katie's room…"

"What's in the house?"

The nurse came into the room.

"I really think Patricia needs to rest now…"

Patricia shook her head.

"In the house in Katie's room, down the hall by the window."

The nurse turned to me.

"Please, that's enough. You're upsetting her."

I opened my mouth to say something, and she pointed to the hall.

"Don't make me call security."

I left. My mind blossomed with the new information. Katie, not Patricia. Was it possible to think that Katie's secret about her sister was not just her sister but that Katie, a clear-headed, bright twelve-year-old child at that, had taken her parents' life and for what reason I couldn't even begin to imagine? But I knew James had stumbled across a very big secret, most likely Patricia, and afraid of the truth that would unfold, she exploded in rage at James, who filed the restraining order and then tried to make up, but Katie couldn't let him back in after he knew. It was too dangerous, yet she couldn't just let him go. "In the house in Katie's room…"

## Chapter 27

Olivia Bennet was standing with her husband at the front entrance of their mini estate as I approached them, the early morning sunrise a brilliant backdrop of pinks and oranges spilling over the desert hills behind them. Olivia's husband was taller than her by a good foot and had wide square shoulders that made me think of a football player. His skin was a deeper hue than his wife's. They both were dressed down in casual wear. What I figured for pj's, hers were a lilac-colored silk and his were a T-shirt and Adidas pants. Both of them held steaming cups of coffee. For a moment, I hated interrupting their peace and quiet—but only for a second.

"Olivia, nice to see you again."

She offered a cautious smile and motioned to her husband. "This is Arnold."

He shook my hand hesitantly. Neither one of them moved from the open door of their house. I could tell their radar was on high.

"Listen, I'm not sure of how we can be of further help. I feel like you wasted your time driving out here."

Olivia spoke first; Arnold followed.

"My wife told me you visited yesterday you were looking for an old friend."

I nodded.

"Listen, I think she may have left something in this house."

Double blinks from two sets of mocha-colored eyes.

"The house was empty as soon as we got the keys. Really, if there had been anything of relevance, we would have set it aside."

Arnold's eyebrows arched as if he didn't agree with his wife. "There was one piece of furniture."

Olivia sipped the coffee, and her smile broadened.

"Oh yes, an antique dresser with a mirror on top. I fell in love with that piece. Katie left it with a note saying 'Welcome.'"

Olivia shook her head and clicked her tongue.

"Such a nice girl. I could only hope to have a daughter like her one day."

"May I have a look at the dresser and perhaps her old room?"

Olivia looked at me quizzically for a moment. "All right…"

She stepped back, but Arnold wasn't so reluctant. He patted his pocket, and I wondered if for a second he was carrying a concealed weapon.

"If I feel like you're crossing any lines, the police will be the first to be notified."

*Yet you just authorized me to enter your property. I'm sure that will go over well.* I didn't mention the latter and stepped inside. Surprisingly, the couple retreated to the living room to finish their coffee, and I headed up the floral carpeted steps to the second floor. I paused at the oak wood hall and looked down at several white paneled doors. I thought of Patricia's words and let them guide me to the end of the hall and the last door on the right, my best guess at her description of Katie's bedroom. I gulped and padded down the hall; the old brass doorknob creaked as I opened the door.

The room was flooded with sunlight, and two large paned windows looked out across the manufactured stretch of green lawn to the low-lying brown foothills of the Arizona desert. The room itself was unused. Old wallpaper in white and blue daisies peeled in the corners, and more oak floors held a Parisian rug in deep blues and mahoganies. The dresser I figured Olivia had mentioned sat against one wall empty. I could only guess the pair of them were wanting to fill these rooms with tiny tots but had not been blessed, yet I wonder what tragedy that story told. I wandered around the empty room, my hands searching along the paper for any uneven bumps or ridges or anything that would jump out at me. After a long moment, I let out a frustrated sigh, wondering if Patricia had led me on a wild goose chase and then got to my knees, exploring the floorboards, lifting up and rolling the carpet gently, but there wasn't a single slat that gave. I got up and dusted off my knees, my mind going a hundred miles an hour, wondering how they would feel if I started pouring their house upside down. I thought more about Olivia's words and finally walked over to the dresser and finally success—a loose drawer bottom revealed a secret slot, and just inside was a hardbound gray and pink journal. I pulled it out and flipped it open, and the truth stared back at me in cold black metal.

"Please don't get up. You have been kind enough. I'll get out of your hair and let you finish enjoying your morning."

Olivia looked at me.

"Did you find something?"

I paused. "Not exactly…I do have one more question for you: did Katie ever mention her sister?"

The look that flashed across the couple's faces said it all.

"I didn't even know she had a sister."

"Okay, listen, thanks. I'll get out of your hair now. You have been more than kind."

I left them both a tad confused and hurried to my car and back into town, making a phone call along the way.

"Lieutenant, its Michael. I have something I think you may want to check out."

"I'll meet you. I was headed out."

I gave my highway location and hung up. Tossing the phone on the seat, I saw a flash of color and turned my head to the left just in time to see the car speed up alongside me, and in an instant, before I could make sense of the situation, the car rammed into the side of mine. My car swerved as I jolted forward, feeling pain shoot through my head as it slammed into the steering wheel. The car spun violently, kicking up dust and rock along the side of the highway before it slid to a stop. More than a bit dazed and confused, I looked up as a trickle of blood ran down my face and saw Katie standing over me. Our eyes locked, and I knew that she knew.

"Katie—"

It was all I could manage and then I felt the butt of the gun she was holding slam against me, and for a second, the world went black.

"Get out!"

I squinted as the trunk popped open and light blasted my face. It created a halo effect as it pierced the blond hair that fell in platinum waves around her face. Big blue eyes were narrowed with anger, and her lips were pursed as she held the gun at my face. A mere hundred and twenty pounds at most, the black sweatshirt pooled around her frame and fell over her dark-colored blue jeans. Her black boots scuffed the dirt in impatience. No matter the circumstance, Katie was a head turner, and I knew without a doubt how she had gotten James and her accomplice right where she had wanted them, pawns in her very deadly game. I, however, outdid her in height and weight, and I was not moved by her reckless beauty. I was enraged with a throbbing pain in my head that trailed down the side of my face.

"Don't even think about trying anything. I'm a good shot…"

I didn't second-guess that. Even if the guy in the alley who had found his demise shortly after James was her henchman, she was the one in the end that had pulled the trigger on both of them. The landscape was familiar to me—acres of rocky dessert terrain and foothills on the horizon. The sun had long since finished its rotation and was climbing the hill in the distance. My head ached and my mouth tasted dry as I slipped out of the trunk and trudged forward away from the main two-lane highway. I thought of my last convo with the lieutenant and knew I had one more trick up my sleeve that hopefully Katie knew nothing about.

"Walk faster…"

I felt the gun suddenly in the small of my back and the rush of her breath near my neck.

"Don't worry, I've covered all my bases."

All of her bases? A sudden chill coursed up my spine, and I thought of Patricia and hoped and prayed she was safe as Katie pushed the gun hard into the flesh of my back and I winced through the layers of my clothing, I took the moment to swivel around, wondering if I could simply overpower her, being so close to her in that moment. The gun whipped away from me and blasted in a loud pop close to my feet, sending dry earth flying into the air.

"Next time, don't count yourself so lucky."

Katie glared at me, and I reluctantly turned back around and stepped forward, my feet slipping a bit on the uneven rock. I felt her back off a bit but was pretty certain the gun was still aimed at the back of my head.

"Please don't tell me you hurt Patricia."

A sudden cackling laugh bounced off a small piling of rock.

"So now you care about the pore sap too. Don't sweat it—she is not worth my time…anymore at least!"

I tried a desperate angle. "James cared about you, he really did…please don't…"

"Don't give me any of your therapist bullshit. What is it called, reverse psychology?"

We stopped at the shallow opening of a couple huge rocks, it looked vaguely like the start of a cave.

"In!"

The gun was pressing back into my backside, and I stepped into the cool alcove, enveloped by darkness once again.

"James found out about Patricia, didn't he?"

I turned around slowly, my heart pounding in my chest. Katie never let the position of the gun waver, and now I was staring down the barrel of the gun. I looked into her blue eyes, filled with a raw fire of emotion. I saw a mirror of her sister there and wondered if they had ever been close or had if Patricia had simply been Katie's pawn from the start.

"Tell me the truth. Did James find out the rest…about you and Patricia and your parents?"

I tried to stop my voice from wavering as it naturally caught in my throat at the presence of fear. Katie's eyes seemed, if possible, to frost over. Her lips went flat and taut over her teeth, and her breathing was labored. Bits of hair moved in rhythm across her face, which gleaned with sweat. There was knowledge and understanding there that transpired between us and also a wondering of how I knew such details.

"Aren't you just a smarty pants? You think you have it all figured out. Why the hell do you think you're in this position? You couldn't keep your nose out of where it didn't belong, just like James!"

Her fingers shook around the gun.

"He still loved you. You were his one biggest mistake."

"Don't say that…don't fucking say that!"

Her voice rose in pitch, bouncing off the rock walls, and I figuratively took a stab in the dark.

"He loved you, and it was wrong. It was wrong to say he was going to leave you after he found out, wasn't it, because it wasn't your fault."

A single tear launched out of her blue eye, and she took one hand off the gun long enough to swipe it away as if it too was betraying her.

"It was their fault!"

"It was always about Patricia and never you. I can't imagine how lost and alone that made you feel, how unloved…"

Her gaze met mine. I looked for a flicker of understanding in herself and in my own understanding. Most kids don't kill their parents over simple jealousy, but in the right diluted mind, one can snap easily. Rage can build and turn deadly, and if one sister was already mentally unstable…well, I bet all my cards on that.

"They deserved what they got that day and so did Patricia!"

I stepped in the opposite direction.

"James gave you all that love back and more. After that, he tried to make it up to you, didn't he? He came by with the roses, but it was all too late, wasn't it? The damage had been done. How could you not hate him for that? And it wasn't the order of protection you hated him for—it was because your secret wasn't a secret anymore. He ruined everything, and I don't mean your relationship, I mean your life. He deserved what he got, didn't he?"

The tears came in a torrent now, streaming down her cheeks and not just her hands, but the gun shook.

"We could have had everything if he hadn't been so foolish, if he hadn't found out, if he had just kept things the way they were. Did he ruin everything? You have no idea how much I loved him, and I was going to make damn sure no one else did…and I will keep it that way."

She paused for a ragged breath.

"You don't know what it's like when everything is broken, when it all falls down. I lost everything once, I wasn't going to again…"

The tears subsided, and anger flushed in her cheeks. Her hands stopped shaking as my heart started pounding. I squeezed my eyes shut. I felt everything and nothing all at once. Had it seriously come down to this moment? Was it all going to end like this?

"Put the weapon down!"

The voice thundered at us, and I opened my eyes to see several police officers crouched down, taking what little shelter they could behind the jagged rocks, guns drawn and pointed at Katie. The officer in the lead barked his command again, and Katie turned the weapon away from me and slowly turned around, aiming at the officer.

"Katie, don't. It doesn't have to end like this!" I pleaded with her. I swallowed hard, my hands still raised. I contemplated my next move as Katie stood in a standoff, her gun drawn her finger ready to squeeze the trigger. Knowing exactly how the officers would react and knowing it was all she wanted in that moment, I leapt forward and tackled her from behind. She went down hard, and the gun slipped from her fingers clattering across the rocks. She screamed out at me as I used my height and weight to hold her down. One officer secured the weapon, while another swooped in to secure her.

"Are you all right?"

Two officers escorted Katie away toward a squad car as another attended to me. As the adrenaline ran out of my veins, I began to shake. Except for a few scratches on my palms, I was unharmed.

"Took you long enough."

I looked at Sheriff Wilcox and winked. He grabbed my arm and helped me onto my feet.

"Come on, I'm sure I can find you a Band-Aid in the car."

I laughed.

"I think I need more than a Band-Aid after all that."

I followed him toward the line of squad cars, just a few feet down from the mangled front end of my poor car and the well-dented blue

Honda. I saw Katie was secured in the back of the patrol car, and our eyes met, and then she looked away out the other window. I turned back to Wilcox car and allowed him to wipe my shredded palms with a wipe. I winced as he placed a couple of seemingly unnecessary Band-Aids on the largest of the scrapes.

"How did you know?"

I looked up at him.

"When I saw your car and then Honda, I ran the plates. I also got a second phone call from your friend. She keeps quite the tabs on you."

I shared a painful laugh with him.

"Come on, I'll show you."

The squad cars began to depart, and I walked unsteadily back to my vehicle.

"You sure you don't need to be checked out?"

"I'm fine, just a couple bruises."

I popped open the undented passenger door and tucked my phone in my pocket where it sat on the floorboard. Retrieving the diary as well, I opened the hollowed-out book. The revolver looked back at both of us.

"Damn!"

"It was in the house the whole time. It was in Katie's desk she left when she sold the house."

The lieutenant took the book gently, and we headed back to his squad car. I paused for a moment. One more question still burned quietly in my mind.

"I wonder why she did it?"

The lieutenant tapped the book.

"Time will tell. I can't see any reason, not from the Katie I knew, but how well do we know anyone?"

"True."

I stepped into the back of the squad car, ready to return to the station and give another statement, a right statement this time. I only had one pending question burning in the back of my brain, and that was *Why?* Why had Katie ended her parents' life in such a brutal and calculated way and used her sister as a scapegoat? I almost thought Katie would take that one to her grave. As we pulled away from the mangled wreck of the two cars, I felt my phone vibrate in my pocket. My body broken and bruised and my emotions rattled, I smiled warmly when I saw his number flash across the screen.

"Hey, how are things?"

I sighed. "I'm okay. Yeah, I think so. How do you know to call at the right time?"

A long, low laugh rustled across the line.

"Mmmm, I just wanted to hear your voice. Michael, I miss you. I really miss you, and I don't think I knew how much till I saw your face again."

I sighed and leaned against the windowpane of the squad car. There wasn't a part of my body that didn't hurt more than my heart suddenly ached in that moment.

"I really miss you too."

The squad car bounced off the rocks and pulled onto the main highway. My body swayed gently as I closed my eyes and leaned back against the seat, letting his voice fill me completely.

\* \* \*

Katie Pearson would never see the outside world again. Instead, she would live the remainder of her days inside prison walls courtesy of the Washington State Corrections facility. She had bypassed the death penalty and received two consecutive life sentences for the men she had killed in Seattle. She would stand a separate trial later in Arizona for her parents' murder, though I had reason to believe that would be overturned. Gray Mountain would forever hold secrets only Katie had the answer to.

# About the Author

Sally Kammerer resides in Silverdale, Washington, with her husband, retired army officer Michael Kammerer, and their three children, William, Matilda, and Henry. Sally has studied at Campbell University in Bueis Creek, North Carolina, where she earned a BAS in psychology. She is an active member of her community and church, and when she is not writing, she enjoys hiking and spending quality time with her husband and children.

CPSIA information can be obtained
at www.ICGtesting.com
Printed in the USA
LVHW090057290520
656808LV00005B/417